'Have you ha

Like his propositi
startled her. In her
things. They rep
much else.

'Hardly any compared with your tally, I should imagine.'

He caught hold of her hand. 'What makes you think I'm a womaniser?'

'Because that's the way you come over.'

'Time isn't on my side, Sarah,' Neal said gently. 'The slow approach isn't practical in these circumstances. You're leaving town... It will be a month after that before I get back to the UK. Between now and then, anything could happen. My motto is "seize the day".'

'Mine is "look before you leap"...especially before you leap into bed with someone.'

Dear Reader

I was married in the spring. After the honeymoon, my husband had to leave for a rather dangerous place on the other side of the world. I'll never forget how the months dragged until, just before Christmas, I was able to join him and, as a bonus, found the inspiration for my first book.

The inspiration for SLEEPLESS NIGHTS came in a somewhat similar way. My husband and son decided to climb a mountain in the Himalayas together. They left at the end of September and for the next four weeks I tried not to worry about them.

At last came the night when I flew to Nepal to wait for them there. I reached Kathmandu late the following day, spending another restless night in probably the most bizarre bedroom I shall ever sleep in. Early next morning I went out to explore the city, soon losing my way in a warren of fascinating back streets. Eventually I returned to base. 'Key not here,' said the smiling Nepalese desk clerk. 'Maid cleaning now.'

But it wasn't the maid in my room. It was a pair of hollow-cheeked, bearded climbers who, by hitching a lift on a Russian helicopter, had arrived in Kathmandu a day sooner than planned.

Our joyful reunion was followed by a family holiday exploring the Kathmandu valley until it was time for our son to return to the mountains, this time as one of the organisers of the Everest Marathon. Flying back to Europe, I read my travel notes. Ideas began to form. I hope you will enjoy the story based on that trip as much as I enjoyed living it.

Anne Weale

SLEEPLESS NIGHTS

BY
ANNE WEALE

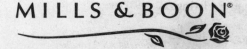

MILLS & BOON®

First published in Great Britain 1999
Harlequin Mills & Boon Limited,
Eton House, 18-24 Paradise Road, Richmond, Surrey TW9 1SR

© Anne Weale 1999

ISBN 0 263 81501 3

Set in Times Roman 10¼ on 11¼ pt.
02-9903-55902 C1

Printed and bound in Norway
by AIT Trondheim AS, Trondheim

CHAPTER ONE

'IF YOU meet a truly gorgeous guy out there and he starts coming on strong, don't back off.'

Giving Sarah her final pep talk, her best friend Naomi went on, 'Life isn't a dress rehearsal. You've got this fantastic chance to break out of the cage. Make the most of it. Around here men to die for are thin on the ground...non-existent would be more accurate.'

Taking Sarah's agreement for granted, Naomi continued, 'In Nepal there's a better supply...or there was the year I was there. Real men like uncomfortable places...oceans and jungles and mountains. When did you last see a ten-out-of-ten in a shopping mall? Never...or hardly ever. They're like any other rare species. If you want to get close to them, you have to go to their habitat...and it's not where you and I are spending our lives, that's for sure,' she added, with a crack of ironic laughter.

Forty-eight hours later, while the airbus droned through the night sky, over mountains and deserts, Sarah was thinking about Naomi's theory that most people spent their lives caged by forces and circumstances beyond their control. Sometimes their conditions were miserable and they were very unhappy. Sometimes the cages were comfortable, even luxurious but, despite that, lifestyles they couldn't escape and which often didn't fulfil their real needs.

Naomi's and Sarah's cages were somewhere between those extremes. Their lives weren't the way they would have liked them to be. Unable to change them, they made the best of them. Until, suddenly and unexpectedly, the door of Sarah's cage had opened.

Now here she was, flying free in an unfamiliar environment that would become more exotic as the adventure progressed.

For two weeks she was on her own, free of all her usual responsibilities...free to be her real self...whoever that real self was.

The woman in the seat next to hers was asleep. From their conversation during dinner, Sarah knew that her neighbour was an off-duty air stewardess for whom flying round the world to glamorous destinations was an everyday routine.

Sarah had never been anywhere glamorous. She was too excited to close her eyes for a moment. They had boarded the aircraft at ten o'clock. Dinner had been served at midnight. After watching both the in-flight movies, she spent the rest of the night reading a guidebook until dawn came up and breakfast was served. Soon after breakfast they landed at Doha, a place that until very recently she had never even heard of.

The stewardess sitting next to her, who worked for an Arab airline and lived at Doha, was looking forward to relaxing in the bath at her apartment in the city. For Sarah it would be another five hours' flying time before she reached her destination. Meanwhile the next ninety minutes would be spent in the airport's transit lounge.

After saying goodbye and thank you to the cabin crew lined up by the door, Sarah stepped out into the dazzling sunlight of a Middle Eastern morning.

Yesterday, in England, it had been cold and wet, a foretaste of approaching winter. Here, in Qatar, an oil-rich desert state on the Persian Gulf, even at this early hour it was already as warm as a summer heatwave in Europe.

Her only luggage was a small backpack. When it had been through the security X-ray machine, she slung it over one shoulder and went in search of the women's room.

She wanted a more leisurely freshen-up than had been possible with so many passengers waiting outside the aircraft's cramped washroom.

Her reflection in the mirror behind the hand basins was startlingly different from the image she was accustomed to seeing in her bedroom mirror at home. Bulldozed into changing her hair colour as well as its style, and advised what to wear and what to pack by Naomi, who had also lent her some clothes, Sarah wasn't yet used to her new image. Or to the feel of the trekking boots on her feet.

She had worn them for part of every day for the past month. But they still felt heavy and clumpy. And what could look more incongruous than a pair of thick-soled boots below the swirling hem of an ankle-length floral skirt in vivid Impressionist colours?

Naomi had assured her that where Sarah was going such an outfit was commonplace. No one would look twice at it, let alone stare in astonishment.

Uncrushable, easily washable long skirts had replaced the thick tweed skirts preferred by the intrepid Victorian lady travellers of a hundred years earlier.

On her top half Sarah was wearing a long-sleeved cotton shirt. Under it was a T-shirt belonging to her friend. Embroidered on the chest was the name of a mountainous route Naomi had trekked with a boyfriend during her gap year between school and college.

Sarah took off both shirts. If any Arab ladies came into the washroom, she hoped it wouldn't offend them to see her stripped down to her comfortable sports bra. Already she had been in transit for a total of twelve hours on her body clock. A proper wash would refresh her for the second stage of the journey.

Fifteen minutes later, wearing only the faded blue T-shirt and feeling surprisingly wide awake despite her sleepless night, she returned to the lounge. Several important-looking Arabs in immaculately-laundered white robes and traditional red and white head-dresses were walking about, but most people were in western dress ranging from business suits to clean or scruffy jeans.

Sarah found the departure gate for her next flight and looked for a vacant seat near it. As she sat down she was aware of her fellow travellers looking her over with the speculative curiosity of people expecting to spend the next week or two in the company of strangers.

Only one person wasn't eyeing her. The man in the seat directly opposite hers was deep in a book.

With a bookworm's instinctive interest in other people's choice of reading, Sarah tried to make out the title. That he was reading rather than gawking at her earned him points in her estimation.

Then she noticed he had other things beside the book to recommend him. Tall, broad-shouldered and long-legged, he was wearing a khaki shirt and trousers with reinforced knees and lots of extra zipped pockets. As he had no luggage with him, apart from a plastic bag from the duty free shop at Heathrow airport, she concluded he was carrying all his vital belongings on his person, with most of his baggage going in the aircraft's hold, to be reclaimed when they landed.

His lean and muscular build suggested he might be a climber heading for the snow-bound peaks of the Himalaya. Mountaineering and trekking were two of the reasons why foreigners visited the kingdom of Nepal and its romantic-sounding capital, Kathmandu.

Sarah had already noticed that most of the male transit passengers were in need of a shave. But not the man with the book. As darkly-tanned as those of a desert Arab, his cheeks and chin showed no trace of stubble. Everything about him looked spruce from the polished sheen of his boots to the scrubbed-clean fingernails on the strong brown hand holding the paperback.

He looked, she thought, as if he would smell good. Not

from expensive lotions, but in the natural way that clean babies and sun-dried laundry smelled good.

As she was thinking this, and noting the way his thick black hair sprang from a high broad forehead, he glanced up and caught her studying him.

Her instinct was to look away but she found that she couldn't. Something about the steely grey gaze focused on her made it impossible to avert her eyes. For several seconds their glances seemed to be locked. Then, a slight smile curling his mouth, he looked her over as closely and appreciatively as she had inspected him.

'*If you meet a truly gorgeous guy out there...*' The memory of Naomi's advice echoed in Sarah's mind.

It was actually the memory of her friend's salty humour, rather than the admonition, that made her begin to smile. Then with a mental 'Why not?' she gave him her friendliest beam before sharing it with some of the people sitting alongside him.

All of them responded with smiles or nods. In fact her initiative seemed to act as an ice-breaker. First the woman next to her asked which tour group she was with and then all the people around them began chatting to each other. All except the man with the book. He continued reading.

When the flight to Kathmandu was called, Neal Kennedy went on reading. Long experience of air travel had taught him not to join the first rush to the departure gate. Even though the shuttle buses on Arab airports were exceptionally spacious, the first two or three buses would be crowded, the last one half-empty. The trip across the tarmac to the aircraft would offer a chance to talk to the attractive woman opposite.

But when he closed the book and looked up, he was surprised to find she had already gone through. Judging by her outfit, he had taken her for someone who knew the ropes as well as he did. Travelling in boots was one of the hallmarks of the wised-up trekker. Any other equipment that went astray in transit was replaceable. A worn-in pair of top quality boots wasn't.

He had noticed her when they came off the flight from London. She had been ahead of him at the security check. He'd watched her walking away towards the washrooms and liked her back view. But maybe seen from the front...

Then he'd forgotten about her until, a while later, he'd glanced up and found her looking him over. Her front view had confirmed his earlier impression of a figure that matched up to everything he liked about women's bodies. Slim but not too slim, all the parts well-proportioned and set off by a graceful posture. Probably influenced by his mother, a leading osteopath, he had a built-in aversion to people who abused their bones by slouching and slumping.

The woman in the colourful skirt wasn't a beauty or even outstandingly pretty. But she had intelligent brown eyes and an irresistible smile of real warmth. He remembered from way back his father telling him that girls with brains in their heads and generous natures were the ones to look out for.

Aged about sixteen then, he hadn't paid much attention. What do parents know about life? was a fairly standard teenage attitude.

In the intervening twenty years he'd learned that his parents were two of the sanest, wisest people he was ever likely to meet. He and his brother and sisters had grown up with the increasingly rare advantage of parents who loved each other and had the kind of marriage that would last as long as they lived.

Between their generation and his, western society had undergone a cultural earthquake. Values and lifestyles had changed. Many people, including himself, thought marriage was on the way out. These days his brother Chris's disastrous marriage seemed more typical than his parents'.

Observing his brother's experience and its aftermath, Neal had decided he wasn't going down that road.

He had five nephews and nieces and numerous god-children. He didn't need children of his own. Nor did he need a wife in the housekeeper-cum-nurse-cum-social secretary sense of the term.

The practicalities of life he could manage by himself, probably more efficiently than many of today's domestically unskilled career women. His mother had raised her sons as well as her daughters on the precept that every adult human being should be able to do their own laundry and cook simple meals.

The only place Neal needed a woman was between the sheets. Even in his twenties he had never been a stud, learning early that relationships which lasted a while, and included some mental rapport as well as physical harmony, were preferable to casual one-nighters. That said, life was about enjoying oneself. If, when he reached Kathmandu, the right kind of woman made it clear she was available, what red-blooded male would prefer to sleep on his own on holiday?

For the second lap of the flight Sarah had requested a window seat on the port side of the plane. Naomi had said this would give her a wonderful view of the Himalaya on the approach to Kathmandu.

When she reached her row, she found a small plump woman in traditional Nepalese costume already occupying the seat that should have been hers. Had she been a European, Sarah might have pointed out the window seat had been allocated to her. But with her minimal grasp of Nepali she let it go, stowing her pack in the overhead locker before sitting down in the centre of the three seats on the left side of the left-hand aisle.

Some time later, among the last to board, the man with the book came strolling along the aisle. After folding his tall frame into the empty seat next to Sarah's, he turned to her and said, 'Hi!'

'Hi!' Suddenly Sarah was glad the Nepalese woman had commandeered the window seat.

The man beside her leaned forward, put his palms together, inclined his head and said something to the woman by the window. Her face wreathed in smiles, her drop earrings bobbing, she responded.

'Was that Nepali you were speaking?' Sarah asked him.

'Yes...but I don't speak it well. Just enough to get by and make the right polite noises.' Feeling around for the ends of his seat belt, he fastened the clasp across his flat stomach and settled his shoulders comfortably against the back rest. 'As we're going to be elbow to elbow until late afternoon, shall we introduce ourselves? I'm Neal Kennedy.'

'Sarah Anderson.'

'Going trekking?'

She nodded. 'Are you?'

'Not this time.' He looked sideways at the emblems machine-embroidered on her T-shirt: three snow-capped peaks surrounded by a double ring of stitching with the name and date of Naomi's trek between them in a contrasting colour. 'Like you, I've been coming to Nepal for a long time, but not always doing the same thing. This time I'm involved with the Everest Marathon.'

Sarah knew she ought to explain the shirt wasn't hers. But somehow she didn't want to...not yet. From the books she had read about trekking, it was clear that the people who did the hard routes, carrying heavy packs in the company of other seasoned trekkers, were inclined to disdain the groups of tourists who, with all the hard slog done for them by porters, had only to cover the ground on the less exacting routes.

Neal Kennedy looked as tough as they came. She didn't want to put him off her right at the start of their acquaintance. Instead of admitting this was her first time, she said, 'Are you a runner? I thought they were usually shorter and more slightly built.'

'They come in all sizes,' he said. 'But no, I'm not one of them. I'm going to report the event. I'm a journalist. What do you do?'

'I work with computers.' Already firmly decided to forget her everyday life until she returned to England, she didn't elaborate. 'Are you a freelance?'

His smile warmed his rather hard eyes. 'You obviously don't read *The Journal*. I'm one of its columnists…and I do some TV and radio.'

The only newspaper Sarah saw regularly, although she seldom read it, was the scandal-stuffed tabloid her mother took. Sarah herself kept up with world events through an Internet news service. But she was aware that *The Journal* was one of England's most respected and independent broadsheets, read by the movers and shakers, the people who mattered. It followed that Neal must be one of the stars of his profession, even if he didn't look at all like her idea of a top journalist.

'I must look out for your column when I get home,' she said, returning his smile.

At close quarters, the parting of her lips and the glimpse of her perfect teeth gave Neal a buzz. He wondered how many men had kissed that passionate mouth and if one had kissed her goodbye at Heathrow last night. The fact that she was alone wasn't conclusive. Even his parents sometimes went on trips separately.

He had already noticed that, although Sarah was wearing several decorative silver rings, her wedding ring finger was bare. Most of the women he knew who had live-in lovers wore a dress ring on that finger to indicate they were in a relationship. Not that being in a relationship necessarily stopped them from having a fling on the side if they felt so inclined and the chance came up.

Neal preferred to stay out of entanglements with other men's girlfriends. Seven or eight years ago a bored and unsatisfied wife had figured in his love life, but her husband had been having affairs of his own for years and couldn't complain at being cuckolded. Neal hadn't repeated the experience. There were more than enough unattached females around to make poaching other guys' women a pointless exercise.

He knew that his determination to steer clear of a serious relationship troubled his parents who wanted him settled down with a wife and family. But he'd managed to avoid losing his heart this far and now was out of the danger zone when the drive to reproduce was at its most powerful, persuading people that what were basically chemical reactions were emotions that would last.

Sitting next to Sarah Anderson, strongly aware of the curves filling out her souvenir T-sheet and the slim thighs outlined by the soft folds of her skirt, he felt the beginnings of arousal. Sensibly, she wasn't wearing one of the heavy cloying scents some women thought seductive but which could be overpowering in confined spaces like aeroplanes. The only fragrance he could catch came from her freshly washed ash blonde hair. The big brown eyes suggested that by nature she was a brunette. But the dye job was subtle, not brassy, and suited her creamy skin. In general he preferred long hair. Hers was cropped boyishly short, possibly styled for the trek. A pair of dramatic silver earrings were set off by her long graceful neck.

The plane was starting to taxi towards the runway. As she turned her head to look out of the window, he wondered how she'd react if he leaned over and put his mouth to her nape by a charming little flat brown beauty spot.

He had no intention of doing it…not yet. But it amused him to speculate how she would take it. Although it was rare for physical attraction not to be mutual, women's responses depended on lots of other factors.

'When are you starting your trek?' he asked.

'Not till Tuesday. After a long flight, a couple of days to relax is a good idea, don't you think? When does the Marathon start?'

'In two weeks, but some of the people will be arriving ahead of time. Kathmandu is a place where I'm always happy to spend time...even though it's changed a lot since you and I first came out.'

His assumption that she shared his familiarity with the city was curiously warming, Sarah found. How she wished it were true. There had been a time when it might have been. With Samarkand and Darjeeling, Kathmandu had been a name ringing with magic for her since she was in her teens. There had been many others and by now she might have seen them all if it hadn't been for... Her mind shied away from the thought.

The aircraft was taking off. It was smaller than the previous one and not as full. When the pre-lunch drinks trolley came round and Sarah asked for a gin and tonic, the stewardess explained apologetically that this was a 'dry' flight.

'Just the tonic, then, please.'

Neal had the same but asked for two extra glasses. Why became clear a little later when the trolley had moved on and he bent down to retrieve the plastic carrier shoved under the sheet in front of him when he sat down.

'My laptop and my liquor supply,' he explained, showing her its contents, a black portable computer and a half bottle of gin.

'Aren't you afraid your laptop will be damaged without proper protection?'

'It's a lot less likely to be stolen. Those fancy padded bags that businessmen flaunt are like women's handbags.

They shout a message to thieves—''Here it is...come and get it!'' I noticed in the airport that you had a small shoulder bag as well as your backpack. I bet you're not carrying anything vital in it.'

'No, I'm not,' she agreed. Naomi had given her a zipped cotton bag on a loop which went over her belt. The bag slipped under her skirt and lay snugly against the side of her tummy. It held most of her money, her credit card and a copy of her passport.

Neal filled both the extra glasses with a generous measure of gin, placed one on her tray and topped it up with tonic. Then he did the same with his. *'Om mani padme hum,'* he said, raising his glass.

She didn't have to ask him what the words meant. They were a Buddhist mantra meaning 'The jewel at the heart of the lotus'. She was interested in Buddhism, having a personal reason for hoping that death was not an end but, as Buddhists believed, the threshold of another lifetime on the long journey to enlightenment.

Neal didn't miss the expression that flickered across her face. He wondered if she disapproved of him using the mantra as a toast. Or if the words had reminded her of something she didn't want to remember.

During lunch he tried to draw her out about her job. But she didn't want to be drawn and he turned the conversation to books, his yardstick for judging whether a woman would be an interesting companion when they weren't making love.

Sarah scored high. She had read every travel book he mentioned and some he had missed. It turned out they had both recently re-read James Hilton's *Lost Horizon*, a big best-seller in the Thirties and one of the few novels to put a new word, Shangri-la, into the language.

'My grandfather gave it to me for my twelfth birthday,' said Neal. 'When did you first read it?'

Her lovely smile lit up her face. 'The Christmas before

my fifteenth birthday. I used to spend my pocket money in a second-hand bookshop. Mr King, the old man who owned it, gave me *Lost Horizon* as a present because I was the youngest of his "regulars".' Her smile faded, replaced by a look of remembered anguish. "He died of bronchitis that winter and the shop never reopened. I missed him terribly.'

After a pause, she added, 'When I discussed the book with him, Mr King said there might really be a place like Shangri-la...a secret valley in the mountains where people lived to great ages and were fulfilled and contented. For a while I believed him. But if such a place had existed, it would have been seen by now on a satellite photograph. Still, it's a lovely idea.'

'My grandfather says that Shangri-la does exist,' said Neal. 'But not as it is in the book...a mysterious, inaccessible place somewhere on the great plateau of central Asia. According to him Shangri-la's in the mind. It's possible for everyone to find it, but not many do.'

'How old is your grandfather?'

'Ninety next year, but still amazingly active and up to date...spends a lot of his time surfing the Web and e-mailing other old men whose minds are still in good shape.'

She laughed. 'Good for him.'

But she didn't volunteer any information about her family, he noticed. Given the smallest encouragement, most people talked non-stop about themselves. A recent example had been the elderly woman who had sat next to him on the Underground from central London to the airport. Starting from a comment about the size of his pack, she had gone on to tell him the medical details of her husband's last illness followed by a detailed character assassination of her only son's second wife.

In contrast to that woman's garrulity, Sarah was telling

him nothing about her family background. There had to be a reason for her unusual reserve.

After lunch, the Nepalese woman turned to Sarah and murmured, 'Penny.'

It wasn't hard to guess what she meant. Sarah turned to Neal. 'My neighbour wants to go to the washroom.'

He rose, stepping into the aisle, and she followed. While the Nepalese woman went to the nearest bathroom, they stayed on their feet, glad to stand up for a while.

'I wonder if that's the limit of her English vocabulary...Pepsi and penny?' said Sarah, remembering the woman's response when the stewardess had asked if she wanted a drink before lunch. 'My grasp of Nepali isn't much better...only about ten words.'

'Nowadays not many tourists bother to mug up any,' Neal said dryly. 'I always try to learn a smattering of the language before I go somewhere new.'

Looming over her in the narrow space between the rows of seats, he seemed even taller and broader than he'd looked when she first saw him. It was unusual, she thought, to find physical power allied to an intellectual turn of mind. It turned out the book she had seen him reading was a collection of essays by Edmund Burke.

Shortly after they resumed their seats, a small child, aged about three and of indeterminate sex, started running up and down the aisle. After a while it suddenly lost its bearings and began to howl, 'Dadee...Dadee...'

Perhaps the toddler's father was catching up on some lost sleep and wasn't aware that his offspring was in a panic. Daddy failed to materialise and all the cabin crew seemed to be taking a break.

As Sarah heard the wails coming closer to where she was sitting, she was about to leap up when Neal forestalled her. Scooping the little thing up and holding it under its armpits, he started to walk down the aisle, saying something quietly reassuring and holding it aloft.

Sarah moved into his seat to watch him, thinking inconsequentially that he looked very good from the rear, wide shoulders tapering down to narrow male hips and a taut and sexy backside.

Then, far down near the front of the cabin, she saw him restoring the child to its parent. Quickly she returned to her own seat, faintly surprised that he alone, of all the people in the nearby aisle seats, had taken action to stop the frightened bawling. For the first time it struck her that he might be married with children of his own.

'You dealt with that very expertly,' she said, when he came back.

'I have a nephew that size.' After a pause he added, 'My preference is for children you can hand back to their parents when you've had enough of them. Journalism and domesticity don't go well together.'

'I suppose not,' she agreed, wondering if that was a warning. If so, it was bordering on arrogance to consider one necessary at this stage of their acquaintance.

On the other hand he was definitely as close to Naomi's mythical ten-out-of-ten gorgeous male as she was ever likely to meet. Maybe experience had taught him to make it plain from the outset that anything he had to offer would be strictly short term and no strings.

The movie was followed by afternoon tea. Sarah's first intimation that they were approaching Nepal was when the woman beside her leant forward to peer out of the window. This meant that Sarah could see very little which was terribly disappointing. Had she had the window seat herself, she would have made a point of keeping well back to allow her neighbours to share the first sight of the famous mountains. Still, it was the little woman's country they were approaching, she reminded herself, and who had more right to gaze on those amazing summits than a returning Nepalese?

Perhaps Neal sensed her frustration. He touched the woman's arm, speaking to her in a way that sounded far more fluent than the polite noises he had claimed were his limit. After that she pulled back and they were all able to see the Abode of Snows, which was what Himalaya meant, gleaming like white cake icing in the late afternoon sunlight.

When that distant view of the great peaks changed to a close-up view of the green hills surrounding the Kathmandu valley, Sarah knew the excitement she would have felt at being close to the point of meeting her trekking companions was tempered by reluctance to say goodbye to her present travelling companion.

Neal, aware of the fact that she hadn't slept between London and Doha, said suddenly, 'Tonight you'll be tired before you're halfway through dinner, but how about meeting tomorrow night?'

'I'd like to...but it could be difficult. Could I call you in the morning?'

'Sure...I'll give you my number.' He produced a pad of Post-it notes from one of his many pockets and a pen from another. After scribbling some details, he peeled off a note and handed it to her. 'Make it before nine, will you? I have a lot to do tomorrow.'

Sarah decided to say, 'I hope I can make it. I'd like to.'

'I'd like it too...very much. I've enjoyed talking to you.'

The subtext implied by the smile that accompanied this statement made her insides turn over. But was she mad even to think of taking this further? It was all very well for Naomi to lecture her about not backing off, but Sarah's every instinct told her that, in this instance, her friend's advice could be dangerous.

*   *   *

They were inside the airport when he touched her for the first time.

Naomi had told Sarah that everyone on incoming flights had to join one of two line-ups. Sarah had obtained her visa before coming but would still need to have it checked. Neal had told her he preferred to buy his visa on arrival. After that everyone had to buy some Nepalese money from an exchange desk because it was not obtainable outside the kingdom.

When they came to the parting of the ways, Neal held out his hand, taking her smaller fingers in a firm but not crushing grip. The contact sent an electric reaction right up to her armpit.

'Until tomorrow night.' He obviously took it for granted that nothing was going to stand in the way of their date.

His assurance irked her a little, but she let it pass. 'Goodbye, Neal.' Turning away, she knew that, if she had any sense, in the morning she would ring him and tell him she couldn't make it.

She needed a man in her life, had needed one for a long time. But for all kinds of reasons, she didn't need a man like Neal Kennedy.

From what she had already learned about him—not to mention all he didn't yet know about her—they were wrong for each other in every possible way.

CHAPTER TWO

SITTING at the back of the mini-bus, with a garland of fresh marigolds round her neck, Sarah studied the guide who had come to meet the thirteen trekkers and shepherd them through the chaos of touts and taxi-drivers waiting outside the airport building.

The guide had introduced herself as Sandy, a suitably androgynous name for someone who had a few female characteristics but whose general appearance and manner was more masculine than feminine. Sarah, who didn't usually dislike people on sight, had felt an instinctive aversion to the woman who now was standing next to the driver and lecturing them with the aid of a microphone. Lecturing was the operative word.

Did she really expect them to take in all this stuff before they had caught up on their sleep? Sarah wondered. It would have made more sense to hand out a printed supplement to the bumph they'd already received. But perhaps Sandy liked the sound of her own voice and believed in making it clear from the outset that she was the boss of this outfit and they had better remember it.

Surreptitiously checking out her fellow-trekkers, Sarah felt her spirits sinking. She had expected a lively group of fit, mixed-age and mixed-sex adventurers. But even allowing for the fact that they'd just come off a thirteen-hour flight and were not at their best, without exception this lot were older, more out of condition and, to be blunt, duller than she had anticipated. Suburban was the label that sprang to mind when, in ones and twos, they had assembled round Sandy after reclaiming their baggage.

As provincial suburbia was where Sarah had spent her

entire life, the last thing she wanted was to spend the next two weeks with people from the same unexciting background. Which of the other single women, she wondered, was to be her room-mate and tent-mate?

She found out half an hour later when the mini-bus entered the forecourt of a large hotel and numerous uniformed porters began unloading the baggage.

As each trekker stepped off the bus, Sandy re-checked who they were, gave them a name badge and, except in the case of the couples, told them who was their 'partner'. Sarah's partner was Beatrice, a thin woman in her sixties whose pursed-lips smile was more like the grimace of someone who had just swallowed a spoonful of disgusting medicine.

The view from the window of their room made Sarah feel more cheerful. Beyond the rooftops of the city was part of the ring of mountains enclosing the Kathmandu valley, with glimpses of higher peaks in the background.

'I can't believe I'm really here at last,' she said dreamily, leaning on the sill, enraptured.

When Beatrice didn't respond, she looked over her shoulder. Her room-mate had started unpacking. Looking up for a moment, the older woman said, 'I hope you're a tidy person, Miss Anderson...or do you prefer to be called Ms?' Her tone held a thread of sarcasm.

How to make friends and influence people! Sarah thought incredulously. Aloud, she said pleasantly, 'I prefer to be called Sarah. I'm going to go down and order myself a stiff pick-me-up, leaving you to arrange your things in peace. As we seem to have only one key, perhaps when you've finished up here you'll come and find me. See you later.'

Although the daylight was waning and it wouldn't be long to sunset, she had her drink in the hotel's well-kept garden. Even the five-star hotel was a bit disappointing, being international rather than Nepalese in style. She had hoped for somewhere with more character.

Wondering where Neal was staying, she remembered the note she'd attached to the inside cover of the notebook she'd bought for a travel diary. He had written his name, the name of his hotel and the telephone number, all in the neat capital letters of someone for whom accuracy was essential and facts were sacred...or should be, she thought.

Less than an hour ago she had been determined to steer clear of any more encounters with Neal. But now she had changed her mind. If, as it turned out, she was going to be stuck with Sandy, Beatrice and the rest, an evening with Neal would at least be an interesting send-off. In fact she could hardly wait for tomorrow morning to call him and fix it.

Soon after eight, while Beatrice was downstairs having breakfast, she rang him from the hotel bedroom.

'Putting you through,' said the operator.

'Neal Kennedy.' His voice sounded even deeper and more resonant on the telephone.

'It's Sarah. Good morning.'

'Good morning. Had a good night?'

'Fine,' she said untruthfully. 'And you?'

'I woke up at four and read. It takes a couple of days for my body clock to adjust. Can we have dinner tonight?'

'That would be lovely.'

'I'll pick you up at six-thirty. We'll go for a drink at the Yak and Yeti beforehand.'

Sarah knew from her guide book that it was Kathmandu's largest and smartest hotel. She said doubt-fully, 'I didn't bring my little black dress.'

'No problem. Rich locals and the world-tour crowd dress up, but climbers and serious trekkers don't. They're not into competitive dressing. Whatever you wear, you'll look great.'

'OK…if you say so. See you later. Goodbye.' As she replaced the receiver, she felt a resurgence of the excitement she had expected to feel every day, every moment. But dinner and breakfast conversations with some of the others, and a night in a room with Beatrice, had quenched that expectation.

She was in the lobby, watching the comings and goings, when Neal strode through the entrance and went to the desk. She knew they would direct him to where she was sitting so she watched him for the few moments he had to wait for one of the desk clerks to be free.

He was wearing the same trousers he had travelled in but with a different shirt. Over his arm he had one of the warm light garments known as a fleece. Naomi had lent Sarah a canary-yellow fleece. Neal's was dark blue with a coral-coloured collar.

He looked strikingly different from all the people in her trekking group. An almost tangible aura of vitality and virility emanated from his tall, upright figure. When, on the clerk's instructions, he swung round and headed for where she was sitting, she felt the force of it even more strongly.

She was on her feet by the time he reached her. 'Ready and waiting,' he said approvingly. 'I hate kicking my heels for half an hour. Let's go, shall we?'

Preceding him out of the door, Sarah smiled at and thanked the saluting doorman.

'Our transport's outside the gate,' said Neal. 'These up-market hotels don't like cycle rickshaws lowering the tone of their entrances. What do you think of this place?'

'I wouldn't have chosen it. A guest house is more my style.'

That morning, on Sandy's guided tour of the city, Sarah

had seen many pedal-driven rickshaws weaving their way in and out of the chaotic traffic. The driver of the one waiting for them was a small thin man with grey hair who didn't look as if he had the strength to pedal two large Europeans. She smiled at him. *'Namaste.'*

'Namaste, madam.' Beaming and bowing, he indicated a metal bar she could use as a step.

The rickshaw's seat was quite high off the ground and designed for people of smaller proportions than Westerners. When Neal swung up beside her the whole vehicle swayed. It swayed even more alarmingly when, after pedalling a short distance, the driver changed traffic lanes to negotiate a busy roundabout. Glancing down, Sarah saw the wheel on her side wobbling as if at any moment it might fly off and send the rickshaw crashing under the wheels of the cars all around them. Perched on little more than a padded ledge, she had never felt more at risk.

Suddenly Neal shifted his position to put an arm round her shoulders and draw her against him. 'Scary, isn't it? The traffic gets worse every year.'

Leaning into the solid wall of his chest, with his hand firmly spread round her upper arm, she felt a lot more secure. Not exactly relaxed, but no longer unsafe. She liked him for pretending that holding her close made him feel better too. She felt it would take a lot more than Kathmandu traffic to scare him.

Presently the driver turned off the main road down a tree-shadowed side street. Soon this passed through a small shopping centre before arriving at the imposing entrance to the Yak and Yeti.

It was many times larger than the hotel where she was staying, with a palatial foyer giving glimpses of an arcade of elegant shops to the left, a restaurant on a mezzanine level and, to the right, a large bar.

His fingers light on her elbow, Neal steered her past the

pianist playing background music to a table close to the windows overlooking the garden, its darkness illumined by lights outlining the shape of a temple-style pavilion and a free-form swimming pool.

'What would you like to drink?' he asked, handing her the drinks menu.

The bar offered various specialities ranging from an Everest Ice Fall to a Yak's Tail and a Yeti's Smile, but Sarah was wary of cocktails which might pack a lethal punch.

'May I have a Campari and soda?' she asked as a waiter approached.

Neal repeated her request and ordered a beer for himself.

'So what have you been doing on your first day?'

'This morning we had a tour, led by our guide, and this afternoon we were free to do our own thing. I think most of the group had naps. The average age has to be sixty...maybe sixty-five because two couples who've come together are in their seventies.'

'Are they in good shape for their age?'

She shook her head. 'I'm amazed they've all chosen this type of holiday. The rest of them are paying customers. I'm the only one who's on a freebie. When Sandy announced at dinner last night that I'd won the trip as a prize there were a few beady looks...especially as the prize was given by *Stars and Celebs* magazine which specialises in scandals.'

'How did that come about?' Neal asked, raising an eyebrow.

'Someone who likes doing competitions thought the prize would appeal to me and filled in my name on the form. Actually the winner had a choice of three activity holidays. I could have gone snorkelling in the Cayman islands or skiing at Aspen, Colorado.'

'Are you wishing you'd opted for one of those?' he asked.

'I don't ski and I'm not very good in the water. This was the trip I wanted. The group may turn out to be more fun as I get to know them better.'

'I shouldn't bank on it,' said Neal. 'I've always found my first impressions are pretty near the mark. Is Sandy a man or a woman?'

'A mannish woman.'

He frowned. 'Has she put you in her tent?'

'No, I'm sharing with Beatrice who seems to suspect me of being a radical feminist and who snores all night long. I don't suppose it will keep me awake once we're spending long, strenuous days out of doors, but it did last night.'

'But she's not likely to make a pass at you?'

'Definitely not! I don't think Sandy would either. She might put me on a charge for insubordination,' Sarah said, smiling.

He was asking about the other members of the group when a woman's voice exclaimed, 'Neal...I didn't know you were in town!'

He rose to his feet. 'Hello, Julia. How are you?'

'Great...and you?' As she asked, she offered her cheek.

She was almost as tall as he was, model-thin, with a cloud of red hair framing her angular face. Her brilliant blue-green eyes were her only claim to beauty, but she exuded personality.

Neal put his hands on her shoulders and kissed her on both cheeks. 'I'm fine...flew in yesterday. This is Sarah. We met on the plane.'

'Hello.' Julia offered her hand. Her grip was unexpectedly strong.

'Will you join us?' Neal asked.

'Thanks, but I can't. I'm just back from Lukla and still on duty. Tonight's the end-of-trek booze-up. My lot will

be down in a minute.' She looked in the direction of the
lobby. 'I can see one of them now. How long are you here
for?'

'Till the start of the Everest Marathon.'

'Oh, great...we can get together later. Bye for now.'
Her smile included Sarah. She strode away, booted and
jeaned but with a clingy mohair sweater on her top half,
its softness outlining a bosom as surprising as her hand-
shake. Those voluptuous curves above the waist didn't
match the boyish hips and greyhound legs.

'Julia's an outdoor pursuits instructor and a trekking
guide,' said Neal. 'A very tough lady indeed.' His tone
was admiring. 'We met on a course about five or six years
ago.'

'What sort of course?' Sarah asked.

'We were learning how to handle four-wheel-drive ve-
hicles in wilderness terrain. She was the only woman and
by far the best driver. That didn't go down too well with
some of the guys,' he added, with reminiscent amusement.

'But it didn't bother you?'

'I have hang-ups like everyone else...but that isn't one
of them. If a woman handles a car better than I do, it
doesn't hurt my ego. When my parents go out together,
it's always my mother who drives. She enjoys it. My father doesn't. The traditional demarcation lines have always been flexible in our family.'

How different from mine, Sarah thought, before shifting
the conversation into a safer zone by asking if the course
had been a preparation for an expedition.

'In Julia's case, yes. Not in mine. It just seemed a skill
that might come in useful some time.'

When they left the bar, about half an hour later, they
passed Julia and her group. They looked a much livelier
lot than Sandy's charges. Although she was talking as they
passed, Julia appeared to sense that Neal was nearby.

Without breaking off what she was saying, she looked round and waved to him.

The gesture left Sarah feeling that, although it might not apply now, at some stage in their acquaintance they had been close...very close.

'Shall we walk to the restaurant? It's not far if we take some short-cuts,' Neal suggested.

He appeared to know the city like the back of his hand, steering her down dark alleys she would have avoided had she been on her own.

The restaurant was in one of the busy thoroughfares. A signboard *Simply Shutters* indicated its presence but, on her own, she might not have found the entrance which was through a shadowy passage and up a flight of stairs.

The interior of the place was in marked contrast to the somewhat seedy way in. Inside it was immaculate, the tables decorated with fresh flowers, the young waiters informally dressed in Lacoste shirts with long white aprons.

Neal and Sarah were welcomed by the proprietor, a good-looking Nepalese who spoke perfect English and made pleasant conversation while seeing them settled at their table.

His restaurant was small but stylish and the people already there, although foreigners, did not appear to be tourists but residents of Kathmandu, perhaps working at the various embassies or with foreign aid organisations.

The menu was written on a blackboard and Sarah chose the walnut and mushroom roast. Neal ordered Spanish pork.

'How long have you been a vegetarian?' he asked her.

'I'm not...I just feel in the mood for walnuts and mushrooms.'

'You had a vegetarian meal on the plane.'

'How observant of you to notice. But I suppose that's an essential qualification for a journalist. I ordered vegetarian meals when I booked my flight because somebody

told me they're usually more interesting than ordinary airline food.' She wondered if this revealed she wasn't as
experienced a traveller as he assumed her to be.

'Some people think the kosher meals are the best,' he
said. 'A colleague of mine did a behind-the-scenes feature
on the food preparation at Heathrow. The logistics are
mind-bending. British Airways alone needs around
twenty-five thousand meals for its long-haul flights.'

The reminder that he came from the world of newspapers, a far more exciting milieu than her own humdrum
background, made Sarah wonder how long it would take
him to suss out that she wasn't the kind of sophisticated
career woman he was used to.

Racking her brains to contribute something amusing to
the conversation, she thanked her stars that she had a
friend like Naomi who was good at telling jokes and anecdotes. Her own forte—if it could be called that—was
listening rather than talking. But by borrowing from
Naomi's repertoire, she managed to make him laugh a
couple of times.

Towards the end of the meal, when they had both eaten
generous helpings of ginger and apple pudding and were
finishing the white wine, he said, 'Instead of spending another night listening to Beatrice's snores, why not come
back to my place? I don't snore and the room I've been
given is a double with a vast bed and its own roof garden
where I had breakfast this morning.'

The suggestion took Sarah's breath away. She had been
propositioned before, but never so soon or so openly. The
others had done it obliquely, testing the ground before
they came to the point which, with two exceptions, had
never actually been reached because she had made it clear
she wasn't interested.

This time she *was* interested, but it was too
soon...much too soon. Some women might jump into bed
with a man within thirty-six hours of meeting him. Some

might do it even sooner. But sex to her could never be something trivial...a fleeting pleasure to be enjoyed and forgotten.

'I'm sorry...no,' she said awkwardly. 'I wouldn't have come if I'd realised that was what you expected.' To her chagrin, she found herself blushing.

'I didn't expect it,' he said easily. 'It just seems a good idea. If you don't agree, that's OK. I wasn't sure that you would. Women usually take longer to make up their mind about these things. Maybe you're already spoken for.'

'If I were, I wouldn't be here, having dinner with you.' After a pause, she added, 'If that sounds very old-fashioned, that's the way we are where I come from. Small-town, provincial England is several light years behind what goes on in London.'

'Slightly behind...not that far,' Neal answered dryly. 'In big cities there are fewer people watching and gossiping. Small-town people tend to be more discreet, but they're still human beings. My grandfather's favourite axiom is "Love, lust and heartache are part of the human condition. Always have been, always will be." He should know. He's been around a long time.'

'But it wasn't the way it is now when he was a young man,' said Sarah, remembering her father's attitudes. And he had been decades younger than Neal's grandfather.

Neal said, 'Grandpa likes life the way it is now. There's less hypocrisy. The whole set-up is less rigid.'

She was tempted to say, 'My father thought it was too slack, that morals had gone down the drain.' But that was an area of her life she didn't want to expose to him.

The uncomfortable truth of the matter was that she would prefer to keep almost everything about herself under wraps, knowing that, if she laid all the facts on the line, he would disappear...fast.

Instead of coffee, she was having jasmine tea. Neal had asked for hot chocolate. Her tea was set before her with

ceremonious precision by the waiter. She smiled at him.
'Thank you.'

A few moments later Neal said quietly, 'I like the way
you relate to people…not treating them like robots.'
Before she could answer, he added, 'What are you doing
tomorrow?'

'We're being taken to see a couple of temples.'

'Are you free in the evening? We could do this
again…at a different restaurant.'

'I have to stay with the group. There's a slide show and
final briefing.'

'You'd have more fun at Rumdoodles.'

'What's Rumdoodles?'

He lifted a mobile black eyebrow. 'You haven't been
there? It's a bar-cum-restaurant where climbers go to cel-
ebrate…the home of The Summiteers' Club. The ceiling
and walls are covered with cardboard cutouts of yetis' feet
signed by climbers and trekkers who've done expeditions
together. The most famous signatures are Tenzing
Norgay's and Sir Edmund Hillary's. I wonder who *was*
the first to set foot on the summit of Everest…the Sherpa
or the New Zealander? Not that it matters. It was a fantastic achievement.'

It occurred to her that, as well as being a well-known
journalist, he might be an outstanding climber. He certainly had the physique for it.

'Have you done it?' she asked. 'Climbed Everest, I
mean?'

The planes of his face seemed to harden. His mouth
became a grim line. For a moment he looked close to
anger. 'I'm not a mountaineer.' The answer was clipped
and curt. 'There are too many people going up there, paying huge sums of money and putting others at risk in order
to boast that they did it. The mountain is being degraded.'

She could see that although it was he who had brought

up the subject, somehow her innocent question had touched him on a raw spot.

Or was it that, despite his seemingly amiable acceptance of her refusal to sleep with him, he was piqued that she wasn't going to give him another chance to persuade her into bed with him?

Neal signalled to their waiter that he wished for the bill.

'Please let me pay my share,' said Sarah, before it arrived.

'Certainly not. You're my guest,' he said firmly, the reply accompanied by a smile that made her feel foolish for suggesting it.

Outside the restaurant a hopeful rickshaw driver was eager to be hired but Neal declined his inviting gestures.

'We'll walk back, if that's all right with you,' he said to Sarah.

'It's fine with me. Some exercise would be good after all that delicious food.'

Although it wasn't late, already the streets were quieter with many shops closed or closing, giving the impression that before long everyone local would have retired for the night.

The byways through which he led her were even quieter. Suddenly, in a poorly lit lane with the brighter lights of a main road about fifty yards ahead, he put a hand on her arm and drew her to a halt.

'We're nearly back to your hotel. I'll see you to the door but say goodnight here.'

Before she realised what he meant, she was in his arms being kissed.

It was a long time since her last kiss and it hadn't been anything like this. The man had been only a little taller than she was and had spent most of his life in a car or behind a desk. She had not felt herself overpowered, as she did now, by a superior force which, even though it wasn't trying to subdue her, made her feel disturbingly helpless.

Nor had the other man's mouth taken possession of hers with the same confident assurance that his kiss would be welcome. He had not been sure of himself. Put off by his lack of confidence, she had pushed him away.

Neal didn't give her the option of accepting or rejecting his kiss. He held her securely against him, one arm round her waist and his other hand cradling her head while he made it clear to them both that he wanted to make love to her...and knew that she wanted it too but wasn't ready to admit it.

It was so long since she had experienced such feelings that Sarah had almost forgotten how it felt to be swept away by the overwhelming emotions surging through her body now. She was intensely conscious of the tall, strong frame of the man who was pressing her to him.

She had thought that desire was over for her. That never again would she feel the wild, wanton longings she had once felt, with such disastrous results. But now, long dormant but not dead, they sprang into eager life as she felt the hard wall of his chest against her breasts, and the muscular breadth of his shoulders under her wandering hands.

'Are you sure you won't change your mind?'

The question was a husky murmur as he released her lips to explore, with his, the smooth texture of her cheek.

'Let me go, Neal...please.'

With the flat of her hands, she attempted to make space between them, and, surprisingly, succeeded.

He did as she asked, stepping back and dropping his arms. 'If you insist...though I can't think why,' he said sardonically. 'It isn't what you really want. It certainly isn't what I want.'

She combed her hair with her fingers, trying to ignore the tingling and throbbing inside her. 'We're strangers...we've only just met. You may not mind that. I do.

Attraction isn't enough for me. I need to know people…trust them…before I—' She left the sentence unfinished.

'Trust is instinctive, like attraction,' he answered. 'All the important reactions we feel in our bones before our brains get to work. But if you want to postpone the pleasures in store for us, that's your privilege.'

'Men can take the pleasures for granted. Women can't,' she retorted somewhat tartly, remembering a relationship that hadn't worked out. She began to move on.

'I can't argue with that,' he said dryly. 'But I think you know in your bones that it wouldn't be like that for us.'

'My bones aren't always reliable.'

'Have you had many lovers?'

Like his proposition at the table, the question startled her. In her world people didn't ask such things. They repressed their curiosity…and much else.

'Hardly any compared with your tally, I should imagine.'

He caught hold of her hand. 'What makes you think I'm a womaniser?'

Knowing she wouldn't be able to disengage her fingers unless he chose to let her, she said crossly, 'Because that's the way you come over.'

'Time isn't on my side, Sarah,' he said gently. 'The slow approach isn't practical in these circumstances. You're leaving town the day after tomorrow. By the time you come back, I shan't have much time left. It will be a month after that before I get back to the UK. Between now and then, anything could happen. My motto is ''seize the day''.'

'Mine is ''look before you leap''…especially before you leap into bed with someone.'

'Are you naturally cautious, or has life made you that way?'

'Most people get more sensible as they get older.'

How old did he think she was? she wondered. She knew she looked younger than her age because a lot of people expressed surprise when they found out what it was. All the things she had been through hadn't left their marks on her skin as they did to some women. The ash-blonde look didn't hide any threads of grey like the colour rinses of some of her stressed-out contemporaries.

'Were you ever not sensible?' he asked, on a teasing note.

'Oh, yes,' she said, her tone wry. 'At seventeen I was as crazy as they come.' Crazy to break free. Madly in love. 'But that was a long time ago.'

They had come to the gateway to her hotel. Still holding her hand, he came with her to the building's imposing entrance.

'If you decide to skip the official programme tomorrow night, you know where to contact me.'

In full view of the uniformed doorman who had already opened the door and was saluting, Neal lifted her hand and brushed a light kiss on the back of it. 'Goodnight, Sarah. I hope we'll meet again.'

He said goodnight in Nepali to the doorman before turning and striding away, leaving her staring after him, half-tempted to call him back.

But she didn't and moments later, without looking round, Neal went out of the gate and disappeared.

Sarah spent the free morning before the group's departure by air to Lukla wandering round town, grappling with the realisation that she didn't really want to go. She wanted to see Neal again more than she wanted to do the trek. Perhaps she would have felt differently if the others in the group had been more congenial. But they weren't, and she knew that situation wasn't going to improve with closer acquaintance.

After a while she went into the garden behind Pilgrims

Book House and ordered a pot of jasmine tea. There were not many people there that morning but presently another woman on her own wandered in and sat down not far from Sarah. She looked interesting and Sarah would have liked to start up a conversation but the other woman began writing postcards.

Some time later she rose and hurried in the direction of the lavatories, leaving her pack at the table. Either she was unusually casual about her belongings or her errand was urgent.

While she was gone, more people passed through the garden, either coming from the bookshop or going in by the back way. Sarah kept an eye on the pack. Perhaps there wasn't a high risk that an opportunist thief would steal it, but such things did happen.

Suddenly the pack's owner reappeared, very unsteady on her feet and covered with blood. She reeled back to her table and sank down, looking as if she might pass out at any moment.

At this point a waiter arrived with her order, took in the streams of blood and said worriedly, 'Is there are a problem?'

'Yes, there is,' said Sarah, taking charge. 'This lady needs medical attention. Please call a taxi...quickly.' She bent over the injured woman, trying to determine how seriously she was hurt. 'What happened? Can you tell me?'

'I was sick...it made my head swim...I fell against something hard. I think I knocked myself out. I'm not certain...'

'Don't worry. I'll look after you,' Sarah said reassuringly. Luckily, she had the address of a recommended clinic on a slip of paper in her passport. 'What's your name?'

'Rose Jones.' She burst into tears.

*   *   *

The clinic's waiting room, leading off the reception area, was crowded with people when Sarah and Rose arrived. But, seeing the state Rose was in, the woman on duty at the desk quickly arranged for a colleague to show them to a room at the back of the premises.

'The doctor won't keep you long,' said the second woman.

Rose, by now a bit more composed, sat down and closed her eyes. Sarah looked round the room. In the centre was a high examination couch. Everything was very clean and orderly. She knew that the clinic was staffed by foreign doctors and was famous for its research into the causes and treatment of the illness jokingly known as the Kathmandu Quickstep.

Moments later the door opened and Neal walked in. His left eyebrow shot up in surprise at the sight of Sarah. 'What are you doing here?'

'What are *you* doing here?' she countered.

But already he'd switched his attention to Rose. 'Hello...I'm Dr Kennedy. Let's get you up on the couch and I'll be taking a look while you tell me what happened.'

As he drew her to her feet and assisted her onto the couch, Sarah gaped at him in astonishment. He had told her he was a journalist, a staff writer on *The Journal*. He'd said nothing about being a doctor. Had he misled her deliberately? If so...why?

CHAPTER THREE

ALTHOUGH she had flinched and quivered when Sarah had tried very gently to clean up round the injury, Rose submitted to Neal's examination without any nervous reactions. She repeated her explanation of what had happened and lay still while he worked on the wound.

'It's actually quite superficial,' he told her. 'The vomiting sounds like a food poisoning. Where did you eat last night?'

She told him, describing her meal which had finished with apple pie and curd, as yogurt was called locally.

'Could be the curd,' he said.

Sarah watched him perform various routine tests, including making Rose follow with her eyes the movements of his finger from side to side and from the tip of her nose to a point several feet away from it.

He then asked her what shots she had had before coming to Nepal and when she had last had a tetanus booster.

'Right: the nurse will give you a shot to settle your tummy and then you can rest upstairs for half an hour before going back to your hotel. Take it easy for the rest of the day. Tomorrow you should feel OK,' he told her.

Before leaving the room, he said quietly to Sarah, 'I'll have a word with you later...while she's lying down.'

A few minutes later a nurse came to give Rose an injection. Then, with Sarah following, she helped Rose up two flights of stairs to a small room with a bed in it.

'You won't leave me,' Rose appealed to Sarah, while she was having a blanket spread over her.

'No, I may pop out for a coffee, but I'll be here when you come down,' Sarah promised.

In the light of what Rose had confided on the way to the clinic, she was in no state to be left on her own.

Neal was at the foot of the staircase when Sarah returned to the ground floor. 'We'll go round the corner for a coffee,' he said briskly. 'How did you come to get involved?'

As they left the clinic, Sarah explained what had happened from her point of view.

'Now perhaps you'd explain why you fed me all that stuff about being a journalist,' she finished indignantly.

'I am a journalist...a medical journalist. I qualified as a doctor, then came to the conclusion it would be more useful to write about how to stay healthy rather than spend my time lobbing out pills to people who, in many cases, had wrecked their health either from lack of information or from deliberate disregard of the basic rules of self-preservation,' he added sardonically.

'You didn't say you were on the staff of this clinic.'

'I'm not. I'm a friend of someone who is and as they were under pressure when I came by to tell him something, he asked me to take a look at Rose Jones. Is she here on her own or with friends?'

'She's alone at the moment. She came with her husband. It's their honeymoon...but it's gone wrong. He's somewhere up in the mountains and she's by herself. I gather they had a big row and she came back to Kathmandu on her own.'

'It's not the first time that's happened, and it won't be the last,' Neal said dryly. 'Don't tell me, let me guess. She didn't like the rough and ready conditions in most of the trekking lodges. The very basic amenities were too much for her delicate sensibilities. She'd had no idea how tough it was going to be.'

'I don't think either of them had. They'd done some

fell-walking together and Rose enjoyed that. But this trip went wrong from the moment they arrived. Apparently it was arranged by some people who run a small shop in their home town and have Nepalese connections. Even the hotel in Kathmandu where they spent their first night, and where she's staying now, isn't up to the standard they expected. But I can't understand her husband letting her come back alone.'

'Perhaps he can't understand her being prepared to desert him so soon after marrying him,' said Neal.

Preoccupied by her concern for Rose, and by Neal's revelation that he was a qualified doctor, Sarah had been paying no attention to her surroundings. Only now did she realise that they were in familiar territory. The building looming ahead was the Yak and Yeti where they had come the night before last.

In the bar they sat at the same window table where they had had drinks.

'Coffee…tea…or something stronger?' Neal asked.

'Tea for me, please.' Reminded by where they were of the woman called Julia, she wondered if, yesterday, they had got together.

'It could be tricky contacting Rose's husband,' he said, looking thoughtful. 'Have you any idea when they were due to get back if their trek had gone to plan?'

'I didn't go into that. She was crying…on the verge of hysterics. I just tried to calm her down. I think she was fairly distraught before she threw up and knocked herself out in the loo. It's a nervous-making situation: being alone in a nasty hotel in an unknown city after a major row with your bridegroom.'

Neal said, 'Where did you go for your honeymoon?'

For a few seconds the question fazed her. Then she collected herself and said calmly, 'I've never been on a honeymoon.'

He lifted an eyebrow. 'You surprise me. I would have

guessed that you'd walked up the aisle very young and it hadn't worked out.'

'You would have guessed wrong. Like you I'm a dedicated single.'

'With women who look the way you do that usually means a career conflict. You said you worked with computers. Was that a throwaway reference to something extremely high-powered? Are you a computer scientist at the cutting edge of research?'

Sarah laughed and shook her head. 'I'm the computer equivalent of the man who comes to fix the washing machine or the dishwasher...except that I'm female and I fix personal computers. But I have no idea how to fix Rose's problem. There has to be *some* way to contact her husband, surely?'

'Don't worry about that. I'll look into it. Do you have the time to take her back to her hotel? What time are you leaving town?'

It pleased her that he thought her capable of being a computer scientist and that he hadn't forgotten today was the day the group left.

'Not till after lunch. We're leaving for the airport at two and spending the night at Lukla to start the trek tomorrow.'

Neal leaned towards her, his forearms resting on his knees, his long fingers interlaced. 'I wish you weren't leaving so soon. I feel this is one of those times that "taken at the flood leads on to fortune"...at least in the sense of some memorable days, and possibly nights, together.'

She didn't know how to respond but just then the waiter returned and saved her from saying anything.

She watched him unloading his tray, thinking it far more likely that a brief affair with Neal, rather than leading on to fortune, would fulfil the continuation of that famous quotation and, like so much of her life, be 'bound in shallows and in miseries'.

'When you were here before, did you go to Bhaktapur?' he asked, as the waiter went away.

Sarah knew the moment of truth could not be put off any longer. 'I haven't been here before. This is my first visit. I'm sorry my T-shirt misled you. It was lent me by a friend. But I should have put you right.'

Her confession was followed by a long moment of silence. She could not read his expression. Had the lie by omission made him distrust her?

'Why didn't you?' he asked.

'It's hard to explain. I'm not usually careless with the truth. I suppose I wanted you to see me as someone more interesting than I am. We were strangers on a plane and I thought you might be bored if I admitted to being a "newbie".'

As a journalist, used to computer-speak, he would know that was the somewhat derogatory name given to the inexperienced by those who knew their way around.

'Who makes you feel you're not interesting?' he asked.

'No one...not in my own world. But your world is different. I've read enough to know that real travellers haven't much time for tourists. I'm not even much of a tourist. The truth is I've never been anywhere. This is my first time abroad, can you believe?'

'Considering how comfortable you seem, I do find that hard to believe. When I saw you in the airport at Doha, I took you for someone who'd chalked up a lot of air miles.'

'I wish I had. I always wanted to travel, but my life went another way.' She glanced at her watch. Already it was fifteen minutes since they'd left the clinic. 'We mustn't be too long.' She began to pour out the tea. 'I'm glad I've got it off my chest. I didn't like not being honest with you.'

'As long as you promise not to do it again, I'll forgive you. Only straight answers from now on...agreed?'

For a second or two she hesitated. If she agreed, would he want to open doors she would prefer to keep closed?

Another quotation from Shakespeare came into her head. *This above all: to thine own self be true...thou canst not then be false to any man.*

'Agreed,' she said firmly, handing him a cup of tea. 'Tell me about this place you mentioned...Bhaktapur? What's special about it? I don't think Naomi has been there. She's the friend who lent me the T-shirt and made me wear-in my boots.'

'What's special about Bhaktapur is that it's still the way Khatmandu used to be when the only people who came here were mountaineers and hippies. I don't think Bhaktapur will stay the way it is now. Tourism changes places...always for the worse unfortunately. But right now it's still a magic place. You mustn't go home without seeing it...especially the golden gate. It's not as famous as San Francisco's Golden Gate, but if someone could only see one of them, I'd recommend Bhaktapur's.'

'Having seen both presumably?'

'Yes. I spent a year travelling before I switched careers.'

Sarah was silent, sipping the hot tea and thinking thoughts it would be tactless to disclose to him.

Disconcertingly, he read her mind. 'You're thinking that journalism is a trashy occupation compared with medicine. I've had lots of people put that to me. They forget that if it were not for investigative journalists, a lot of bad things would continue unchecked. Some forms of journalism are tacky, but a free press is still our main safeguard against bad governments and unscrupulous vested interests such as some of the drug manufacturers. Just recently I wrote an exposé of racketeering in cosmetic surgery. It carried more weight coming from a doctor and it certainly warned a lot more women to be careful who they trust their faces and bodies to than I could have done any other way.'

'You're right, of course,' she conceded. 'I hadn't thought it through. My attitude to journalists is coloured by all the bad things we know they do...targeting public figures in the hope of catching them doing something they shouldn't...hounding people at times when they need to be private...concentrating on the horrors and ignoring the good side of life.'

'You've been reading the wrong papers. You must try *The Journal*,' he said, smiling. 'I won't say we never publish anything questionable, but I've been with them for five years and I've never felt moved to resign.'

When they returned to the clinic, Neal led the way upstairs to the room where Rose was lying down. She was dozing but only lightly. Within seconds of him bending over her, she opened her eyes.

'How are you feeling?'

'My head aches.'

'Sarah is going to take you back to your hotel. It's very important that you drink plenty of water because of the shot you had and to clear your system. You need sleep but you also need fluids every time you wake up.'

Rose nodded obediently, but Sarah wondered if she would remember and act on his instructions. It was difficult to judge what kind of person she was in normal life. But the quarrel with her husband, ending with them going in different directions, suggested that neither of them was overburdened with common sense.

Rose was certainly in no state to think about paying for the attention she had received. It was Sarah who, while Neal was ringing for a taxi, asked for the bill.

'Do you have your credit card on you, Rose?'

Rose handed it over and signed the docket when Sarah brought it to where she was sitting. But she took no interest in the amount involved. In Sarah's opinion it was very reasonable.

When, the formalities completed, she rejoined Rose, Neal was with her, saying, 'If you're not feeling OK tomorrow, don't hesitate to come back. I shan't be here, but whoever's on duty will have my notes about you.'

Turning to Sarah, he said, 'I hope the trek goes well. Call me when you get back. Take care.' Putting a hand on her shoulder, he inclined his head to touch his lips to her cheek.

After they had gone, Neal waited until his friend Bill was free and then discussed with him the likelihood of contacting Rose's husband.

Neal and Bill had been medical students together. Bill had been married and was now divorced. After the breakup, he had resigned from a thriving group practice and become a locum, standing in for doctors who were ill or on holiday. There was always plenty of work and he claimed to like living out of a suitcase with frequent changes of scene.

Neal thought he was punishing himself for the failure of his marriage. In Neal's opinion most of the blame for that was the fault of Bill's ex, an ambitious lawyer who had refused to compromise when their careers conflicted. There had always been men who sacrificed their family life to their professional goals. Now women were doing the same thing.

While they were talking, part of Neal's mind was on Sarah. She had come clean about something he had already suspected, but he knew she was still holding back information that would normally have been on the table by now.

What, for instance, was behind that cryptic remark 'but my life went another way'? What was the reason for a perceptible hesitation before she had agreed to give him straight answers from now on?

Each time they met he found her more desirable. He wanted to take her to bed with an impatience he hadn't felt for a long time, if ever. He knew that she wanted it too. When he had kissed her cheek, he had heard her draw in her breath, sensed the quiver that had run through her.

Instinct told him that, behind the low key, level-headed façade, there were pent-up emotions which perhaps had been let loose once and then firmly battened down, or had never been released at all. He wanted to light the fuse that would explode her control over those turbulent feelings.

Rose's hotel didn't seem too bad to Sarah. The entrance was down an alley, the ground floor a budget restaurant. On the way there Rose had complained of 'cooking smells' wafting up the narrow stairs to the bedrooms. To Sarah they were the intriguing aromas of an exotic cuisine.

It depended on one's point of view and since her arrival poor Rose had been seeing everything through the distorting lens of disappointment.

Her bedroom was cramped but clean. Sarah turned down the bed and helped Rose to undress and put on a nightdress. As she lay down, she began to cry again.

'I wish I could go home...I hate it here...it scares me being on my own.'

I can't leave her, Sarah thought. At the moment she's so unbalanced, she might do something crazy.

Aloud, she said, 'I have to make a phone call. I'll ask downstairs if I can use their phone. I shan't be gone long.'

Sandy, when Sarah got through to her, said angrily, 'Where the hell are you? Everyone's started lunch. You should have been back half an hour ago.'

'I'm sorry. There was an emergency. Someone was taken ill and I had to get her to a doctor.'

'Where are you now?' the tour guide demanded curtly.

'I'm at this person's hotel. It's in the centre of Thamel. I don't know the address but it's one of the scruffier back-streets. She's alone and still very distressed. I can't leave her in the lurch. I left my backpack ready before I came out. Can't I meet you at the airport? What's the latest possible time I can check in?'

'Beatrice brought your backpack down with her luggage which was very good of her. No, you can't meet us at the airport. I want everyone on the bus at the time on the schedule. Kindly get back right away. If the woman is sick, the hotel will look after her. She's not your respon-sibility...and you're making it bloody difficult for me to carry out mine,' Sandy expostulated.

Her belligerent tone and her language brought back a rush of memories. Sarah was not prepared to be brow-beaten ever again.

She said coldly, 'In that case don't bother. Cross me off your list. Forget about me. I'll do my own thing from now on. Leave my luggage at the hotel and I'll pick it up later on.'

'You can't do that. You're with us.' Sandy was audibly disconcerted by Sarah's response to her bullying.

'I was...I'm not any more. I've gone off the whole idea. I'd rather stay in Kathmandu.'

'Where are you going to stay? Everywhere's very booked up. If you can find a room, how will you pay for it? *Stars and Celebs* magazine won't fork up. They're only committed to cover your trekking expenses.' There was a note of anxiety in Sandy's voice now. Perhaps she was starting to worry about how the situation would impact on her standing as a guide.

'I'll pay my own way,' Sarah told her. 'My flight back will still be valid.'

Having made the decision, she immediately felt much better, even quite kindly disposed towards the bossy woman at the other end of the line. 'Don't worry. I shan't complain. I'm doing this by my own choice. Have a good time. Goodbye.' She rang off.

Her luck was in. Rose's hotel had a single room on the top floor which was free for the next two nights. During the afternoon, while Rose was in a deep sleep, Sarah retrieved her backpack from the other hotel.

Having missed lunch, she was having a snack in the restaurant when Neal walked in.

He said, 'What are you doing here? You should be at Lukla by now.'

'I opted out. I couldn't leave Rose on her own.' Would he guess that wasn't the only reason for the decision? 'How did you know where to find her?'

'You wrote this address on the form at the clinic...remember? How's she doing?'

'Sleeping most of the time. When she's awake she's weepy. But she hasn't thrown up any more and I'm making sure she drinks plenty.'

'She's lucky you were around to pick up the pieces. What's your situation now? Are you staying where you are?'

'I've moved myself here. It's a lot less expensive than the other place.'

'I must take you down to Freak Street some time. That's where I stayed on my early trips. This area, Thamel, was fields then. But I was still at school the first time, so it's going back a long way.'

'Did your school organise the trip?'

'No, no...I came with my brother. He was four years older and the responsible type. My parents knew he'd keep me out of trouble. By the way I've done what I can to get word to Rose's husband, but frankly it isn't much. When people are "on the hill", they're out of reach...and they can't get back in a hurry even if they want to. Now and then, in extreme emergencies, a helicopter will go in and lift out someone who can afford the expense or has insurance cover. But that doesn't happen often.'

Sarah had not missed the abrupt change of subject or the bleak look in his eyes when he spoke of his brother. Intuition told her that something about his first visit was better forgotten...like her own life at that age.

By now she had finished eating.

'Shall I come up and see Rose?' he suggested.

'Would you? That's very kind. I think it would reassure her.'

Rose wasn't there when they entered her room.

'Must be in the bathroom,' said Sarah, starting to straighten the bedclothes and shake up the pillows.

Neal went to the window and looked out. Moments later they heard the flush and then the door opened and, with an embarrassed squeak, Rose stopped short on the threshold before scuttling back into bed and pulling the bedclothes up to her armpits.

'Hello, Rose. How's the head?' Appearing not to notice her discomfiture at being caught in her nightie, Neal sat on the side of the bed and smiled at her.

'It's a bit better, thank you.'

'That's good.' He reached for the bottle of water on the night table, refilled the glass and handed it to her. 'Keep up the fluid intake. We're doing what we can to contact your husband.'

Her small mouth started to tremble. Her pale blue eyes brimmed with tears.

'Now come on, that's not going to help,' Neal told her kindly. He took some tissues from the box by the bottle and thrust them into her hand. 'Blow your nose and stiffen your lip. One good cry is allowable, but Sarah tells me you've had that. More is over the top. You don't want your guy coming back and finding you with pink eyelids like an albino mouse.'

Rose managed a watery titter but did as he told her.

Watching her, Sarah sensed that now she was somewhat recovered, she found Neal's proximity disturbing. As well she might, thought Sarah. Even when he was wearing his doctor's hat, he was still disturbingly tall and muscular and male. Seeing him sitting on a bed immediately raised conjectures about what he would be like *in* bed with a woman who wasn't his patient.

'How's the tummy now? Settled down?' When Rose nodded, he went on, 'That's good. But even if you feel peckish, I'd give it a rest till tomorrow.' He glanced at his watch, 'I must go. Get some more sleep. See you later.'

When Sarah opened the door for him, he signed for her to step outside.

On the landing, he said, 'If I'd known you were going to be here, I'd have asked you to have dinner with me. Now I've fixed to eat with some local people who might be offended if I changed the arrangement. Can we eat together tomorrow night?'

'I think we should include Rose. I wouldn't feel comfortable leaving her on her own.'

'All right, if you insist...but don't let Rose become a millstone. You're here to enjoy yourself, not to nanny her. A crack on the head and a bout of Kathmandu Quickstep are unpleasant but not life-threatening. Until tomorrow.' He gave the top of her arm a light pat before running down the stairs.

Sarah went to bed early and read a book she had bought in one of the many used book shops catering to backpackers.

She couldn't help wondering if the 'local people' Neal had mentioned included the woman called Julia.

As the hotel didn't have room service, next morning, after checking that Rose was feeling better, Sarah brought her breakfast on a tray. Rose decided to stay where she was until lunchtime, reading a magazine.

'I have some things to do, but I'll be back for lunch. I've seen several rooftop restaurants that look nice places to eat,' said Sarah. 'You'll need to stay with bland food for a day or two.'

She had already noticed more than one office where people could pick up and send e-mail and use the Internet. During the morning she went into one and asked what it would cost to use these facilities. The charges being reasonable, she paid the necessary rupiahs and was shown the PC she could use.

She debated spending her first few minutes on-line sending an e-mail to Naomi, but decided against it. She didn't want to explain why she was still in Kathmandu. She would do that when she got back.

Instead she used a search engine to locate the address of *The Journal*. Once she had it, it didn't take long to bring the newspaper's home page onto the screen and to access that day's edition. Neal's column wasn't listed in the index, but it was the work of minutes to trawl through recent back issues until she spotted his name under the heading *Compulsive shopping may be sign of depression*.

A click on the mouse brought the article on screen with a photograph of Neal at the top of it.

When she had read the article, she said to the man in charge of the office, 'Would it be possible to print a copy of this?'

'Certainly, madam. For that I must charge you extra, but the service is very cheap considering we have the very latest technology. Would you like a cup of coffee?'

Touched by his efforts to compete with the cybercafés of the western world, Sarah declined the coffee which would probably be cold by the time it was brought from a nearby restaurant. Instead she took the print-out to the rooftop where she thought they might lunch.

Sitting under a sunbrella, in a booth formed by flowering shrubs, she read Neal's article about shopaholics.

It was a well-written piece, infused with understanding tolerance. If she had never met him, she would have liked the way he came over. Although, if there hadn't been a photograph of him, she would have thought him much older; a man with a long experience of human foibles and a humorous eye for the absurdities of people's behaviour.

The article ended with an amusing paragraph inspired by something he had read in a medical journal. In a study of forty-two doctors' pens, Austrian pathologists found more than half of them infected by at least one type of bacterium. Several other studies had revealed that colonies of bacteria could grow on doctors' ties, which was why they tended to wear bow-ties more often than other men.

The photograph allowed Sarah to study his face more closely than she ever could when he was with her. It was a fine face, as well as a good-looking one, she thought.

But the fact remained that, despite the many good impressions she had of him, she still felt that for a man of his age to be unmarried suggested that, if not an out and out womaniser, he wasn't prepared to commit himself to any one woman.

A couple of hours later when she was sitting in the same chair but this time with Rose on the other side of the table, she said, 'Did you realise that Neal Kennedy is quite famous? He writes a weekly medical column in *The Journal*.'

'Really? When he came yesterday, I had a feeling I'd seen him somewhere before, but I don't see how I can have done. Nobody I know takes *The Journal*. It's a boring paper.'

'You might have seen him on TV. He is on it sometimes, he told me.'

'Oh, is he?' said Rose, showing more interest. Clearly, in her estimation, appearances on television counted for a lot more than being a broadsheet columnist. 'I wonder what programmes he's been on?'

'Ask him,' said Sarah. 'Do you like him?' she added.

'I don't know. I haven't thought about it. I'm too worried about Cliff. Supposing he's had an accident? Supposing he doesn't get back in time for our flight? I wish I'd never let him persuade me to come. I never wanted to come here. I wanted to go to Florida.'

By the end of lunch, Sarah had lost patience with her.

Neal took her to dine at an Indian restaurant which they had almost to themselves.

'I thought if you'd had a difficult day you'd like somewhere uncrowded and restful,' he said, when they had finished with the menus and were sipping their pre-dinner drinks.

'What makes you think it was difficult?'

'Wasn't it?'

Their table was lit by a candle in a glass storm shade. The soft upward glow emphasised his strong features and made his eyes seem more piercing.

'It was rather,' she agreed. 'It probably sounds unkind, but I have to admit I was glad when Rose decided she didn't feel up to joining us.'

'Not half as glad as I was,' Neal said dryly. 'I'd already decided she has all the makings of a heart-sinker, if you know what that is?'

Sarah shook her head. 'Explain.'

'It's a name doctors give to the kind of patient who turns up with heart-sinking regularity and who's never cured of their ailments. Sometimes they're malingering, sometimes they can't cope with what life throws at them. I think Rose is in that category.'

'There may be more than meets the eye to this row with Cliff,' Sarah said thoughtfully. 'She told me at lunch that they hadn't lived together like most people do these days. They both lived with their parents and Rose's sound very strait-laced.'

'You think Rose may not have let Cliff make love to her until the knot was tied?' said Neal.

'I think it's possible...even probable. He may have felt the same way if he came from a similar background.'

'There are some sects who still hold that sex before marriage is fornication,' he agreed. 'Did she tell you she belonged to one of them?'

'No, but reading between the lines of what she did say, it wouldn't surprise me if neither of them had a previous experience. They were married the day they flew out which means their wedding night was spent in the air. Nobody, after that journey, arrives full of sparkle. They must have been even more bushed than most people flying in. It's not an ideal start, is it?'

'So you think things had started to go wrong before the going got really tough?'

'It's mostly speculation...but, yes, I do. I think Rose wants Cliff to come back because she's afraid of being alone here. But she may be equally nervous of seeing him again because...well, because he's put her off the most intimate side of their relationship.'

'There's nothing we can do about it...apart from buying them a copy of *The Joy of Sex*.' Neal's expression was more amused than sympathetic. 'If the guy had had any sense, he'd have arranged to spend their first night together in a comfortable hotel. In fact no one in their right mind would choose to go trekking on their honeymoon...not unless they'd been lovers for some time and were both equally keen on strenuous outdoor pursuits.'

She couldn't deny he was right, but felt he was being a bit heartless to make fun of them. Perhaps he had never had any off-putting sexual experience. Sarah had, and although the passing of time had made her look back on them with greater understanding than she had had when they happened, she felt an instinctive sympathy for anyone in a similar predicament.

Rose was rather feeble in some ways. She wasn't a natural survivor who would surmount any set-back that life sent her way. If the pressures were too great, she might even go under. Nevertheless Sarah could empathise with her. So far the honeymoon had been a series of disasters.

Their Chicken Sizzlers arrived, bubbling and steaming in hot cast-iron dishes set inside wooden platters. It wasn't gourmet food but, tasty and filling, it was what most travellers wanted if they had just returned from time in the mountains or had a tough trek ahead of them.

For a short time they ate in silence. Then Neal re-started the conversation by talking about the book he had been reading the night before.

Sarah concluded from this that he must have been on his own. Although she didn't really think him the sort of man who would invite her back to his room one night, and try to bed someone else a night or two later, there were men who behaved like that, and how could she know for sure that he wasn't one of them?

There were moments, and this was one, when she felt as comfortable with him as with someone she'd known for years. But in fact she'd known him for five days and she shouldn't forget it.

They had finished their meal and were at the coffee stage when Neal said, 'If you can't stay where you are after tonight, you'll need to find a new base. Any ideas?'

Sarah felt a small knot of tension tightening inside her. Intuition told her he was about to suggest something which might be a repeat of his previous proposition.

'I'll look around in the morning. I'm sure I'll find somewhere to stay.'

'I'm thinking of going up to Nagarkot for the weekend. It's up in the foothills. People go there to see the sun rise and set on five of the world's highest peaks. There's a converted farmhouse which is a nice place to stay. Would you like to come with me?'

'It sounds lovely...but I'd worry about deserting Rose. I don't think she's fit to be left on her own.'

He didn't try to persuade her to change her mind. Nor did he suggest postponing his trip. Maybe that wasn't a possibility. She didn't know what other commitments he had. Perhaps, having been turned down twice, he wouldn't try again. Even self-confident men didn't like being rebuffed. Who did?

As they strolled back to where she was staying, Neal didn't appear to be annoyed. He talked about the Internet and specifically about the British Medical Association and its website on the Net which could be accessed by anyone in the world who was interested in health and medical science.

Near the entrance to the guest-house, he said, 'Shall we have another drink or some tea?'

'If you'll be my guest,' she said, for again he had refused to let her contribute anything towards the bill at the restaurant.

'OK.'

As they passed the counter, Neal spoke to the man who seemed to be the proprietor of the whole establishment. The reply was much longer than his greeting and accompanied by a gesture at Sarah and another gesture at the ceiling.

Unable to guess what he was saying, she waited for Neal to translate but first he steered her to a table and drew out one of the chairs for her.

'What was that all about?' she asked.

'Cliff has turned up. He arrived about an hour ago. That lets you off the hook.'

He paused for a moment, a challenging glint in his eyes. 'So how about being very brave and coming to Nagarkot with me?'

CHAPTER FOUR

THE implication that she was a faint-hearted person, almost as timorous as Rose, flicked Sarah on one of the most sensitive areas of her *amour propre*.

She lifted her chin and smiled at him. 'Why not? But only on condition we share the expenses.'

'If it'll make you happier.' He switched to the news they had just learned. 'I wonder what's going on upstairs...if they're making love or engaging in fresh hostilities?'

'Let's hope they've discovered they need each other after all. But we shan't find out till tomorrow.'

'Can you be ready by nine? We could stop off at Bhaktapur on the way.'

'Yes, that's no problem. How far away is Nagarkot?'

'Only an hour's drive from here. To hire a car and a driver isn't expensive. He'll take us to the farm and come back to fetch us when we're ready to leave. If the weather is good we could stay longer than the weekend. There are several interesting walks. They'll give you a taste of what Nepal's like in the rural areas.'

Presently he said goodnight, repeating the brief, light kiss he had given her at the clinic.

Neal walked back to his hotel feeling kindly disposed towards Cliff whose opportune return had eliminated Sarah's justification for saying no to a weekend together.

He was gradually piecing together a few details about her background but the picture was mostly blank.

Everything he knew about her he liked. She was good company: intelligent, well-read, amusing.

Her physical allure became stronger each time they met and he was able to study her in more detail. He particularly liked her hands with their short, clear-varnished nails and slim but not fragile wrists. Some women's hands turned him off. The thought of Sarah's hands on his body made him burn with impatience for the weekend ahead.

But whether it would go right from the start, or if there would be problems to overcome, was impossible to tell.

When, earlier tonight, they had been discussing the possibility that Cliff and Rose were sexually incompatible, there had been something in Sarah's expression which suggested to Neal that she had been there before them.

He could have been mistaken, but he didn't think so. His short time in general medical practice had taught him to recognise the signs—sometimes hard to detect—that patients had more on their minds than the physical ailments which had brought them to the surgery.

From his experience as a GP and, more recently, from letters from the readers of his column, he had learnt that problems with people's sex lives were extremely widespread.

But, if he was right about Sarah, he felt sure the blame for whatever had gone wrong didn't lie with her but with her partner or partners. As she had said when he was walking her home from *Simply Shutters*, men could take it for granted there would be some pleasure for them, if not always the maximum. But a woman locked into a relationship with a lousy lover could spend her whole life missing out.

Back at his hotel, he picked up his key, passed the crowded bar and the lifts and went up the stairs two at a time, aware that he was looking forward to tomorrow with a keener anticipation than he could remember feeling for a long time.

By the time they came back from Nagarkot, he expected to have the answers to all the things about Sarah that puzzled him.

In his room, he took off his clothes, thinking about undressing her, remembering the enticing little mole at the nape of her neck he had seen on the plane.

It had been luck that put them on the same aircraft. But it hadn't, as she might imagine, been luck that put them next to each other. The seat assigned to him had been several rows further back. Being among the last to board, he had known it was unlikely that anyone would claim the vacant seat next to hers.

He realised now that he had wanted her from the moment in Doha airport when he had looked up from his book and found her watching him. Although she might never admit it, she had felt the same way. What was going to happen at Nagarkot had been inevitable from their first exchange of glances.

What he had to make clear beyond any possibility of misunderstanding on her part was that a great weekend was just that and nothing more. They would have a great time together, two independent adults in what had to be one of the world's most glorious locations.

Afterwards...well, it would probably last for the rest of her time here. But when it was time to say goodbye, that would be the end of it. Because relationships started when people were on holiday hardly ever survived the transition to everyday life. And even if that had not been proven many times, his life was already organised the way he wanted it. There was no permanent place in it for a woman. He had decided that a long time ago.

At eight the next morning Sarah went down to have breakfast in the restaurant and settle her bill. She had expected to have a restless night but after lying awake for about half an hour, thinking about the decision she had made, she had slept soundly till woken by the minuscule alarm clock bought specially for this trip.

She was eating a bowl of muesli and curd when a stocky young man with prematurely thin hair and a fair skin reddened by an overdose of sun appeared in the doorway with Rose.

Sarah put down her spoon and went over to say hello. 'You must be Cliff. I'm Sarah. I was hoping to meet you before I left.'

'You've found somewhere else to stay?' Rose asked.

'No, I'm leaving Kathmandu. Neal is taking me to see Bhaktapur and then we're going up to Nagarkot, in the hills to the north.'

Before Rose could respond to this information, Cliff said, 'My wife's been telling me how kind you've been. I'm very grateful.'

Sarah smiled at him. 'It was no more than anyone would do in the circumstances. I'm glad you're back. I wouldn't have been happy about leaving if Rose had been on her own, but we heard last night you'd turned up. Will you join me?'—with a gesture at her table.

From their manner and conversation as they had breakfast with her, she gathered that being apart had made them realise they had acted too hastily in splitting up. Rose kept looking at him so fondly that Sarah began to feel she must have been wrong in surmising that Cliff was a clumsy lover. Or it might be that Rose's need for someone to protect her in an alien environment outweighed her distaste for that side of their relationship. As Naomi was fond of saying, there were still plenty of women who, just to have a man in their lives, focused their minds on something else while their partners were satisfying needs they didn't share or enjoy.

Thinking about the man who shortly was coming to fetch her, and the days and nights ahead, Sarah lost track of the conversation. She was pulled back to the present by the realisation that Cliff had asked her a question she hadn't heard because her mind was full of Neal.

At the same moment Neal himself entered the restaurant, making her insides do somersaults at the sight of his tall, authoritative figure and distinguished looks.

There being no time to apologise for woolgathering while Cliff was asking whatever it was he had asked, she jumped up, saying, 'Please excuse me. I haven't paid my bill yet.'

To Neal, moments later, she said, 'Good morning. I'll run up and get my pack and then pay what I owe. It shouldn't take more than five minutes. Why not have a few words with Rose's husband? They're over there.'

After glancing in their direction, Neal looked down at her again, saying, 'You haven't changed your mind, then?'

'Did you expect me to?'

'I hoped you wouldn't, but it's a woman's privilege.'

'Once I've made a decision I stick to it,' Sarah said lightly. 'Shan't be long.'

As the hired car stopped at a junction where the narrow, congested streets of Thamel joined one of the wider, faster roads, Neal said, 'If it's all right with you, we'll postpone the visit to Bhaktapur and go there on the way down. I feel like relaxing in the country and you've probably had enough of the city for a while, haven't you?'

'Some peace and quiet would be good,' she agreed, wondering if there was another reason for rearranging their itinerary. 'What did you think of Cliff?'

'I should say they're pretty well matched. I wouldn't want to be stuck on a desert island with either of them.'

They were sitting behind the driver. Neal reached out a hand to take hold of one of hers and draw it onto the stretch of seat between them where he continued to hold it. 'With you that situation could be fun.'

Wondering how much, if any, of this conversation the

driver could understand, she said, 'You'd certainly be an asset. A doctor is useful anywhere and everywhere.'

He laced his fingers with hers and the ball of his thumb moved gently over the back of her thumb. It was a casual caress but it had a far from casual effect. She felt the latent strength of his fingers and the hard heel of his palm. She knew that, by coming with him, she had given this large but shapely male hand a licence to touch her wherever it pleased. In the most literal sense she had put herself in his hands, to do with her as he wished. For someone who had lived so long without a man, it was a strange sensation.

As they passed out of the city into the country, Neal looked out of the window on his side of the car and Sarah looked out of hers, fascinated by the difference between what she was seeing and the way things were where she came from.

A young woman stood in a doorway, languidly passing a comb through a hip-length cascade of black hair. In the dusty forecourt of an open-fronted shop some small boys were kicking an improvised football made from a tangle of plastic cord. They appeared to be enjoying themselves just as much as the children in her home neighbourhood whose playthings were expensive.

Neal drew her attention to a couple of adolescent girls using a giant swing constructed from bamboo poles lashed together. Their hair and their long skirts fluttered like pennants. They, too, looked as happy—happier than the far more sophisticated teenagers Sarah saw at the bus stop across the road from her house.

Presently the houses became more scattered. The road wound between fields where people were harvesting rice. They passed a girl leading several buffaloes. What Sarah took to be white blossoms in the tops of some trees turned out to be egrets.

'Why is that dog wearing marigolds round its neck?' she asked, as they passed through a village.

Neal spoke to the driver in Nepali. The man looked over his shoulder and smiled at her. 'Today is Dog Day...also Cow Day,' he told her.

Further on they saw more dogs sporting garlands. Gradually the road became steeper and more winding. Eventually they began to see signs with the names of guest houses at the mouths of side tracks.

It was another fifteen minutes of bumpy riding along an ever-narrowing dirt-and-rock track before the driver stopped the car at a place on the side of a wooded hill where there was enough space for him to turn round.

He jumped out and went to open the boot where their packs were. Sarah opened her door and stepped out into the warm mid-morning sunshine. She took a deep breath of the pure greenery-scented air.

'What a lovely spot, but—' gazing around and not seeing any buildings '—where's the farmhouse?'

'Along that path, I suppose?' said Neal, indicating a footway that disappeared round a bend in the hill.

Evidently the driver understood some of this. He nodded, holding the straps of Sarah's backpack for her to slip her arms through. Neal's pack he would have carried although it was too heavy for him to handle with ease. But Neal took it from him, heaving its weight onto one broad shoulder.

After saying goodbye to him, they set out along the path. Not far round the bend was a gate beyond which the path rose more steeply beneath overhanging trees. At the crest of the rise they found themselves at one end of a large garden. At the other stood a two-storey building surrounded by a veranda. A number of people were sitting at easels set up to face in different directions. For on all sides the views were superb: miles of undulating land, much of it terraced and farmed, and, in the distance, a vast panorama of mountain peaks.

As Sarah paused to absorb this first impression, from close behind her Neal said in an undertone, 'Hell! I was hoping we might have the place more or less to ourselves. This lot look like a painting group.'

She smiled at him over her shoulder. 'Don't be so anti-social. If they're artists they'll be interesting people.'

He returned her smile, but his tone was sardonic as he said, 'I doubt if they're professionals, honey. Their tutor may be, but art groups are usually made up of amateurs with more enthusiasm than talent. I've tangled with them before.'

'I haven't, so I'll enjoy it.'

'You're here to tangle with me.'

The glint in his eyes brought a rush of colour to her face. She turned to look at the farm and, hopefully, hide her blush from his amorous grey eyes. Moments earlier his use of the American endearment had sent a small thrill of pleasure through her. Now his last remark had stirred her up even more.

She wondered if he meant to make love to her as soon as they were alone in their room. She was impatient to be kissed again but a little nervous of what would follow the kisses. Unlike Naomi who quite often went away for weekends with men, Sarah was conscious that her own experience didn't amount to much compared with most people's.

As she approached the first of the easels they had to pass on their way to the entrance to the farmhouse, the elderly woman working at it looked up and said, 'Good morning,' her smile embracing them both.

Some of the others were too intent on their work to notice the newcomers. Near the door Sarah stood aside to let Neal take the lead. Swinging the pack off his shoulder, he dumped it on the veranda close to the wall, then stepped inside the building.

Following him, Sarah found herself in a large room with several dining tables, a bar and a wooden staircase leading to the floor above. Behind the bar was the owner or manager of the establishment. Neal was already talking to him in Nepali.

A few minutes later he turned to her. 'The artists are occupying the house. We're in the annexe.'

After re-shouldering his pack, he returned the way they had come, veering off in the direction of a long low building she hadn't previously noticed. With an overhanging thatched roof forming a brick-paved veranda, it was fronted by a strip of grass and a border filled with white and yellow chrysanthemums.

Again Neal dumped his pack, this time next to a door which was standing open but had a cotton screen hanging from inside its lintel and hiding the room within.

'You're in here...Number Six,' he said, taking a key from his pocket and handing it to her. 'I'm next door...Number Seven.'

She was surprised into saying, 'They don't have any double rooms vacant?'

'These are double rooms,' he answered. 'Let's unload our gear and then go and have coffee and maybe something stronger?'

Holding the heavy pack by two canvas handles, he disappeared into the other bedroom.

Baffled by why he should think that, having agreed to come, she would want a separate bedroom, Sarah did as he suggested. Holding aside the screen, she entered a room with sky-blue rafters and a yellow-boarded roof space. The walls were bare brick painted a coppery colour. Between the twin beds, a tiled floor was spread with a Tibetan tiger rug. On the wall was a picture of a holy man with long hair flowing on the ground on which he was sitting. The frame was draped with a white silk scarf.

Exploring the adjoining bathroom, she found it had modern fittings, including a shower and hand basin.

She was unpacking some things from her wash bag when she heard Neal knock on the door frame.

'Come in.' She stepped out of the bathroom as he ducked under the door screen.

'It turns out the views are better than the amenities,' he said.

'They seem fine to me. It's a very nice room.'

'But lacking a clothes closet.'

She shrugged. 'With my wardrobe, a few pegs are good enough. What's the significance of the scarf draped over the picture?'

Because the walls of the bathroom formed a corner with the beds in the area beyond it, Neal had to move to the foot of the beds to see the picture.

'It may have been put there by someone who was presented with a scarf when they left where they were staying before. Scarves like that are a traditional farewell present.'

He sat down on one of the beds and gave it a couple of test-bounces. 'The mattresses don't seem too bad, but I've slept under kapok-filled quilts in other places. They're bulky and heavy, but not warm. The nights are cold at this height. We'll need down sleeping bags. I bought mine and borrowed another.'

Separate rooms and sleeping bags...it wasn't the scenario she had visualised.

Neal beckoned her to him with a crooked forefinger. As she came closer, he stood up. 'I also have two sets of thermal tops and long johns, but I don't think we're going to need them.'

He put his arms round her and kissed her, starting with a butterfly brushing of mouth against mouth and then a break, gradually increasing the pressure until, about six kisses on, he drew her closer against him and kept his lips locked to hers.

Last time it was she who had broken off their embrace. This time, just when she was starting to melt with pleasure, he put her gently away.

'Let's go and find that coffee.'

Trying to work out the conundrum of why he had stopped made her oblivious to the views as they returned to the main house.

The art group were having their coffee break. Like the group Sarah hadn't gone trekking with, they were all well past middle age except for one man about Neal's age, presumably the tutor, who hadn't been around when they arrived.

Spotting two strangers, he detached himself from the others and came over.

'Hi! Where have you people come from?' Before they could answer, he offered Neal his hand. 'I'm Roger Kent...from England.'

'This is Sarah. I'm Neal.' Evidently Neal thought surnames unnecessary and assumed that his accent would make it clear where he came from. 'We've come up from Kathmandu. Have you been here long?'

'Arrived yesterday, staying for three nights,' said the other man. 'I'm in charge...for my sins.' Having his back to the rest of those present, he rolled his eyes and made what was clearly intended to be a comical grimace. Lowering his voice, he added, 'One can overdose on grey panthers, as the Americans call them. Nothing very pantherish about this lot. Hippos would be more apt.'

'Are you an artist or just the group's minder?' Neal asked.

'I'm a pro. They're Saturday painters. Where are you heading from here?'

'We haven't decided yet.' Neal turned to Sarah. 'I'll get

the coffee.' He moved to the bar, leaving her to continue chatting.

'Where are you going next?' she asked.

She wasn't taken by Roger. Although she herself had been put off by the prospect of trekking with people many years her senior, she didn't approve of his making fun of his group to a couple of strangers. Anyway the artists looked a lot more interesting than her fellow trekkers. Their clothes alone revealed them as a bunch of 'characters' and their animated conversation was punctuated by roars of laughter.

'To Bhaktapur,' said Roger. 'Have you been there?'

'Not yet.'

'Fabulous place...one of my favourites.'

He was showing off about his travels when she saw Neal carrying their coffee to another part of the room. As soon as Roger paused for breath, she said, 'Would you excuse me?' and escaped. In addition to being what Naomi would call A Giant Ego, he had an assessing way of looking at her that she didn't like.

Having put their coffee cups on a table in a sitting area reached by a short flight of stairs, Neal was scanning a shelf of books. 'This must be the "library" I was told about,' he said, as she joined him.

'I haven't read that.' She tapped the spine of one of the larger volumes. 'Have you?'

Opening it at random, he held it so she could see the photograph spread across two pages. 'No, I haven't seen this before. Let's have a look through it.'

Sitting elbow to elbow with him at the table, browsing through the beautiful pictures the book contained, Sarah found her attention split between what she was looking at and what she was feeling about the man whose long leg was almost but not quite touching hers.

His kiss had changed her hesitance to impatience. So much of her life had been wasted in vain regret for a long-lost happiness that, had it had time to mature, might not have fulfilled her youthful dreams. She was a different person now, with so much to catch up on, so much to learn. Instinct told her that Neal would be an expert tutor.

The Nepalese man brought them two small glasses of liquor.

'What is this?' she asked, when he had gone.

'Khukri rum. It's the best of the local spirits...good with coffee.' He picked up his glass, tipped half the contents into his cup and lifted the glass toast-fashion. 'To a happy time that we'll both look back on with pleasure when we're my grandfather's age.' He downed the rest of the rum in a single smooth swallow.

Unaccustomed to hard liquor because she couldn't afford it, Sarah sipped it more cautiously. 'Mm...it's smoother than I expected. Wine is what I mainly drink.'

He gave her an appraising look. 'But not very much, by the look of you.'

'How can you tell?'

'Women who knock back a lot tend to have puffiness here—' using his middle finger, he traced a line under one of her eyes '—and dehydrated skin. You don't have either.' His hand brushed her cheek before finding its way round to the back of her neck. 'They've all gone back to their easels.' He leaned forward and kissed her.

Last time her excitement had mounted gradually. This time, in a flash, she was at the pitch where their last embrace had broken off. She wanted to press herself close to him, to have her arms round his neck, her fingers stroking his hair.

At the same time she was inhibited by the fact that, although the painters had gone, the man who had brought their drinks might reappear. Knowing that open displays of affection between men and women were frowned on in Nepal restrained her from responding as eagerly as she wanted to. But even to have her hands on Neal's hard chest was a thrill. He felt as solid as a tree, his body warm through his shirt. But she couldn't feel his heart beating, only her own.

The ringing of a telephone and the patter of feet across the dining area brought the kiss to an end. Neal released her mouth. His hand left the nape of her neck and slid slowly, caressingly along the top of her shoulder and down her arm.

Looking deep into her eyes, he said softly, 'You go to my head.'

She drew in a long breath. 'It's mutual.'

'Then why don't we do something about it?'

Though neither of them had finished their coffee and Sarah's glass of rum was still more than half full, he took her by the hand and led the way up the few steps and out of the building.

They were walking in the direction of the annexe when they were intercepted by Roger. 'I say, are either of you two clued up about malaria?'

Neal frowned at him. 'This isn't a malarial area. The Terai is the only risky part of the country.'

'I know, but one of my people was bitten by a mosquito the evening we arrived and now she's having a shivering fit. I'm not too sure how to deal with it.'

Sarah saw a muscle bunch under the taut brown skin of Neal's jawline. 'Where is she?' he asked curtly.

'Over there.' Roger pointed towards two women, one sitting on a camp stool and the other bending over her.

Neal had already let go of Sarah's hand. 'I'd better take a look,' he said to her.

'Of course.' She followed him across the grass to where the standing woman was speaking in a low tone to the other.

When Neal reached her, he went down on his haunches so that she didn't have to crane up at him. 'You're not feeling well, I hear. What's the problem?'

She gave him an anguished look. Although she was in the sun and wearing several layers of woollies, she was shaking with cold.

'I had a pain in my back...between my shoulder blades. Now I feel terribly cold and I can't stop shivering. Oh, dear, I do hope it's *not* malaria. My grandfather had it all his life. It used to make him feel ghastly.'

'When did the pain in your back start?'

'About an hour ago. I was feeling all right till then...apart from a bit of a cough.'

The other woman spoke. 'Maureen had a bad chest cold a fortnight before we came away. The cough has hung on, but her coughs generally do. She's always been chesty. We're sisters. I'm Delia.'

'My name's Neal. I'm a doctor,' he told them quietly. 'Maureen, you should be in bed. I'll come and listen to your chest when I've fetched various things I need. I'll be there in about five minutes.'

Maureen was able to walk without assistance. As she and her sister headed for the house, Neal beckoned Sarah to accompany him to the annexe.

'I'm sorry about this, but I think she may have pneumonia which, at her age and stuck up here, isn't funny.'

'What makes you sure it isn't malaria? Even though Kathmandu isn't malarial, couldn't a mosquito have hitched a lift from the Terai on somebody's backpack?'

'I suppose that's a possibility, but the time between the mosquito bite and the onset of symptoms is ten days to a fortnight for malignant malaria and longer for quartan malaria. Roger says these people flew in less than a week ago.'

At the door of his room, he said, 'Come in.'

Like her, he hadn't unpacked much. Delving inside the big backpack, he brought out a plastic box and a water-proof drawstring bag.

'How serious is pneumonia?' she asked.

'It used to be very bad news in the days before antibiotics. Now it doesn't usually last long but patients, especially the older ones, may take several weeks to get fully back to normal.'

'What a godsend for them that you're here.'

'But not such a godsend for us,' he said dryly. 'Never mind: we can play doctor and patient later on…after lunch. Lock up for me, will you?' Making a kissing noise at her, he headed back for the house.

On her own, Sarah strolled round the garden, thinking about how if it hadn't been for Rose's accident she probably wouldn't be here, and now she was here the fundamental reason for her coming had been postponed because of someone else's illness.

Her thoughts were interrupted by Roger. 'Do you know what's going on?'

'Neal has some medical knowledge.' She thought he might not want everyone to know the extent of it. 'He's very good when there's trouble. I'm sure he'll know what to do for the best.'

'I hope so. It'll be damned awkward if the old girl has got malaria. She's not a bad artist actually…was at art school a long time ago. But like most women of that generation she gave it all up to wash some guy's socks. Now he's popped off and she's free again, but too late to do serious work. We get a lot of widows on these jaunts.' He gave her a speculative look. 'I'm divorced. How about you?'

Sarah ignored the question. 'It's never too late to exercise talent.'

'What's yours? I'm sure you have one.'

'I'm into clip art.'

Roger looked blank. 'What's that?'

'Stuff people use on computers. Not your sort of art. Excuse me. I'm going to my room.'

She was sitting outside it when Neal came back.

'Is it pneumonia?'

'All the signs say so. Anywhere else but here, I'd send her straight off to X-ray for confirmation. But I'm ninety-nine per cent sure it is pneumonia so I'll get some medication started and she can go down to the clinic tomorrow morning when her fever is down.'

'Have you told Roger?'

He nodded. 'Can't say I take to him. Don't like his attitude.'

'I don't either.' She told him about her conversation with Roger.

'He's probably disappointed that the group doesn't include someone like you,' said Neal. 'Although I should think what he really likes is a gullible twenty-year-old who will swallow his Great Artist act. Some top-class painters do lead these groups, I believe, but I doubt if he's one of them. I've never heard of him. Have you?'

'No, but that doesn't prove anything. I don't know much about contemporary artists.'

Neal glanced at his watch. 'Nearly lunchtime. I'll just put my stuff away and then I'll be with you.'

On the way back to the house, he took her hand, looking down at her with undisguised desire. 'Let's hope this isn't going to turn into one of those French farce situations where every time we're about to make love one of the painters chokes on a bone, or breaks one,' he said dryly.

Sarah laughed. Suddenly she felt wonderful. Not only was she close to the top of the world in the geographical sense, but she felt on a high peak emotionally. To have met 'a truly gorgeous guy' was incredible luck; but a ten-out-of-ten with a sense of humour was something else, as Matthew would say.

She pushed the thought of her son to the back of her mind with everything else she didn't want to think about.

Where she was now, like cyberspace, was an escape from real life. She would have to return there eventually.

Meanwhile she was here, in a place very close to paradise with an afternoon in Neal's arms just a short time away.

Only a fool would let thoughts of where it would end tarnish these golden hours.

CHAPTER FIVE

MOST of the painting group were already seated at the long table when she and Neal entered the house.

He steered her to the round table furthest away from the others. 'Don't expect too much of the food,' he murmured. 'Away from Kathmandu, it's never anything special.'

In Sarah's present state of mind, a bowl of plain boiled rice would have been acceptable. She didn't care what lunch was like. What came afterwards was all she could think about. If he had said, 'Let's forget lunch,' she would have agreed.

Roger came out of a room leading off the main room. Seeing them, he came over. 'Let me buy you a drink. It's the least I can do when you've been so helpful.'

'Thanks, but I've already ordered. Some other time perhaps.' Without being overtly uncivil, Neal's tone managed to convey that they wanted to be on their own.

To Sarah's relief Roger got the message. 'This evening perhaps.' He moved away to join the group.

'And perhaps not,' Neal said softly. With a silent eye-signal, he brought the manager over and spoke to him in Nepali. When their food came, a bottle of white wine came with it.

The main course, a mixture of fried rice and vegetables, reminded him of the time when one of his sisters, then twelve, had stayed with a friend whose mother was a diabolical cook. The good manners instilled by their parents had made Jenny Kennedy feel obliged to force down soggy sprouts, boiled parsnips and watery spinach. When she came home and described this ordeal, her father had rewarded her with a handsome tip to be spent in the place where she spent all her pocket money, a bookshop.

This led on to other anecdotes from Kennedy family life and Sarah knew it would have been normal and natural to reciprocate with stories about her own family. But there weren't any. She had been an only child, born late to middle-aged parents, one with no sense of humour and the other afraid to express it.

It wasn't until she had met Naomi that Sarah had realised she, too, had been repressing a natural inclination to see the funny side of things.

Seeking a conversational substitute, she told Neal about searching for his column on the Internet and asked him about the paper and the mechanics of his job.

Answering Sarah's questions, Neal wondered if it had been idle curiosity or a suspicion that he might not be telling the truth that had prompted her to visit one of Kathmandu's cybershops and verify that he was who he said he was.

The irony of that being that it wasn't he who was being devious but Sarah herself. The only person in her life she had mentioned was her friend and business partner Naomi. All the others, and there had to be others, were a mystery. It could be that she was an orphan, brought up in circumstances she preferred to forget, and that her adult relationships had been similarly unhappy. But somehow he didn't think so.

In every way, except in her curious silence about her domestic background, she came over as a normal, well-adjusted person with none of the tell-tale signs shown by disturbed personalities.

He wondered if she was using a contraceptive pill and had the feeling she wasn't. He didn't know how old she was but could make a fairly accurate guess and a lot of women in her age group were beginning to worry about long-term use of pills and turn to other methods. Either way it didn't matter. He had seen too much of the consequences of unsafe sex ever to risk it himself.

Perhaps later, after they had made love, she would satisfy his curiosity about her.

As the painters finished their meal and either drifted back to their easels or lingered over their coffee, Neal said, 'I'll just check on Maureen. She may not feel like eating yet, but it's important she takes plenty of fluids. Shan't be long.'

Sarah watched him mounting the staircase until only his long legs were visible and then only his trekking boots. When they had disappeared, she sat drinking the last of the wine. They had finished the bottle between them, but it hadn't been potent enough to give her the light-headed feeling she sometimes had when she and Naomi shared a bottle of good wine. Her mind had never felt clearer. She knew she was on the brink of an experience that would change her life for ever even if it had no lasting impact on his.

By the time Neal came down she had finished her wine and was waiting for him near the door.

'How is she?'

'Sleeping. I didn't wake her. I've been talking to Delia outside their room. She's a retired speech therapist...an interesting woman.'

How different from Roger's attitude, thought Sarah. Neal found out about people before he stuck patronising labels on them.

The painters were gathered round Roger who was giving a demo. Neal took Sarah's hand and they walked back towards their rooms. But on the way to the annexe he veered off towards the path by which they had entered the grounds.

'A little stroll before we siesta...OK?'

'Fine by me,' she agreed.

But she couldn't help feeling piqued that now, when there were no more impediments, he didn't seem as eager as she to consummate their relationship.

Hand in hand but not talking they went down the path into the tunnel of greenness where the branches of the surrounding trees formed a canopy. Suddenly Neal halted, pulling her into his arms and kissing her with an ardour that made nonsense of the idea that he wasn't impatient.

'Change of plan,' he said huskily, some moments later. 'We have all tomorrow to explore. Right now...'

Taking her hand again, he began to retrace their steps at a fast stride. Almost running to keep up with him, her lips burning from the heat of his kiss, her heart beating wildly even without the exertion of being hurried uphill at this altitude, Sarah had a moment of *déjà vu*, that peculiar sensation of being in a new situation yet feeling it wasn't the first time that it had happened.

It lasted only a few seconds and there wasn't time to puzzle it out because very soon they were back at the annexe.

'Your place or mine?' Neal asked.

'Yours,' she said breathlessly.

With the door unlocked and pushed open, he ushered her in, then relocked it. Two strides had him drawing the curtains across the wide window.

Oh, God, this is it! thought Sarah, in last-moment panic.

But then she was back in his arms, the irrational alarm replaced by the lovely sensation of being held close to a powerful male body, its latent strength under the control of someone she knew would never use it against her.

At some point in those first feverish kisses he scooped her off her feet and seconds later she was cradled on his lap on one of the beds.

'Mm…you smell delicious,' he murmured, nuzzling her neck.

'You too.' Her hands were enjoying the freedom to explore the structure of his broad shoulders.

'But you have too many clothes on.' He began to get rid of them, starting with her leather belt, opening the buckle and pulling it through the loops on her trousers. Then he unbuttoned the waistband and pulled down the zip, but only to tug her shirt free. He had stopped kissing her and she opened her eyes and watched as he dealt with the buttons on her shirt.

This morning she had decided to replace her sports bra and cotton briefs with a set of more glamorous underpinnings Naomi had insisted she must bring with her 'in case'.

That contingency was happening at this very moment.

'This is pretty.' He touched the flowery georgette of the chain-store camisole, his hand caressing her midriff and then sliding higher to cover one of her breasts. The warmth of his palm through two thin layers of semi-transparent fabric made Sarah draw in her breath.

All the inhibitions she had expected to have evaporated in the urgency of her longing to feel his hands on her bare skin. She sat up and shrugged off her shirt, tossing it aside. Then she grabbed the hem of the camisole and pulled it over her head. Finally she reached behind her and unclipped the georgette bra.

As she freed her arms from the loosened straps, she *did* have a moment of misgiving. What if, when he saw her naked, her body didn't appeal to him? She wasn't a twentysomething with a gorgeous big bouncy bosom to die for. Her breasts were still firm but only 34B.

'Lovely…I knew they would be.'

As Sarah sighed with relief, Neal looked at and touched and tasted her pulsating flesh as if he had never been offered anything more pleasing.

It was difficult to speak, even to breathe, while he was stroking and nibbling, but she managed to gasp, 'I want to touch your chest.'

Reluctantly he stopped what he was doing and leaned back on his hands. 'I'm all yours.'

Still perched on his lap, she slipped the tongue of his braided belt through the buckle but left the belt in the loops of his pants. They were fastened by a metal press stud she found it hard to undo. Supporting his weight on one arm, Neal opened the stud for her. She could feel his gaze flickering over her nudity as she freed his shirt and tackled buttons. When they were all undone, she unwrapped him like a surprise parcel, exposing the most beautiful male chest she had ever seen, or at least the one most appealing to her personal taste.

Instead of being hairy, Neal's skin was smooth and lightly tanned. The first sign of hair began below his navel. His chest, his ribs and the upper part of his belly were as inviting as a polished wood sculpture. Starting from his collarbones, she ran her hands slowly down his body, loving the taut sleek feel of him.

She was repeating the caress, discovering a depth of sensuality she hadn't realised she had, when Neal straightened to take off his shirt. Then he pressed her against himself in the first intimate contact of their half-naked bodies.

'Mm...' The sound she made was like a cat's purr of pleasure.

He answered it with a low growl from somewhere deep in his throat and that made her feel like laughing and, an instant later, like crying. Because this was what she had once had, and lost, and never found again.

'We've forgotten something,' Neal murmured, his lips exploring the curve between her neck and her shoulder, his hands fondling her waist.

'What?'

'We've still got our boots on.'

'Oh.' She saw what he meant. They couldn't take off their trousers until they had shucked their boots. 'Well, in that case...' She slid off his lap onto the bed alongside him and bent to unfasten her laces.

'I like your back.' She felt his lips trailing a kiss down her spine. 'But it's your front I'm crazy about.' From either side of her a warm hand burrowed under her bent body to find and cup her breasts.

'How can I concentrate when you're doing that?' she protested. 'What about *your* boots?'

He laughed and let her go. Although she had started first, his boots were off before hers. He stood up, unzipped his trousers and took them off, to be followed by his underpants. She was aware of all this without looking up from her task. When, her feet bare, she straightened, he was stretched on the other twin bed, waiting for her to join him.

As Sarah rose to step out of her pants, she heard footsteps on the veranda.

'*Oh, no!*' she breathed in dismay.

But whoever it was wasn't about to disturb them. The footsteps passed on to one of the rooms beyond theirs.

'New arrivals perhaps.' Neal held out his arms to her.

Quickly she whipped off the lace-trimmed micro briefs, put one knee on the edge of the bed and sank down to lie against him, aware without actually looking that he was ready to take her.

But it seemed he knew more about women than any of her previous lovers. Without any sign of impatience, he began to kiss her again, first her mouth and then her body. The touch of his lips and tongue on all her most sensitive places was mind-bending. She found herself gripping the sides of the mattress, her body arching with delight as his hands roved over her body with a tender mastery that made her his willing slave.

Very soon she had to use one of her own hands to muffle the whimpers of pleasure she couldn't repress.

'Oh, please…you must stop…I…oh, God!'

The world blacked out, leaving nothing but an exquisite sensation tingling through her entire nervous system.

It was still there, but dying down, when she felt him slide smoothly inside her as if their bodies had joined many times before.

Sarah opened her eyes to see Neal swinging off the bed. She had no time to admire his long brown back and the lighter skin of his sexy male backside before he had disappeared, heading for the bathroom.

Had she been asleep, or merely in a deep torpor induced by being wholly fulfilled for the first and only time in her life?

How come he made love so brilliantly? she wondered. Was it a gift some men had? Or did it come from much practice? Either way it wasn't important. All that mattered was what he had given her: a feeling of completeness that had always been lacking, as if some vital part of her was missing. Now, at long last, she knew that it wasn't.

Neal reappeared, still naked, but not to return to her arms. Pulling the quilt off the other bed, he draped it over the room's only easy chair. Then he came to where she was lying, scooped her into his arms and carried her to the chair, folding the quilt round her.

'What's this in aid of?' she asked.

'To keep you warm while I rearrange the furniture. A single bed's too confining.'

She watched him remove the night table from between the twin beds and push them together. Then he removed all the bedclothes, spread the other quilt across both beds to cover the join and replaced the bedclothes, overlapping the sheets and blankets at the centre.

Watching the movements of his splendid body with its

powerful but not over-developed muscles, Sarah felt an anticipatory frisson at the thought of spending the night with him.

She wasn't expecting him to say, 'Right: now let's start again...without any restrictions.'

What did he mean by that?

'Now?' she said uncertainly.

'No better time than the present.' His eyes were glinting with laughter and more than a hint of devilment.

Aware that knowing all the theory wasn't the same as having hands-on experience, she stayed where she was, reminded of the time at school when she had been dared to jump off the swimming pool's top board and had lost her nerve and chickened out.

Neal came to the chair and put his hands on the arms, leaning over her. When he'd first returned to the bedroom his body had been quiescent. Now he was strongly aroused.

Bending still lower, he gave her a long, lingering, deeply sensual kiss. Before it ended, she knew that this time she wasn't going to lose her nerve. Wherever he led, she would go. The quilt fell away as she put arms round his neck and rose with him as he straightened, pressing herself against him.

They made love, dozed in each other's arms, made love again and slept. When Neal woke her by kissing her eyelids, the dimness of the room told her it was early evening.

'Let's take a shower. I'll go and run the hot water in case it takes time to come through.'

A few moments later she heard the water running and Neal whistling like a man without a care in the world. Too contented and lazy to move, she lay thinking that it felt as if they had been making love for years, not just a few hours. Now they were going to shower together, an experience she expected to be a lot more exciting than the solitary baths she was used to.

'I hate to tell you this, sweet thing, but I think there's a problem with the boiler. The water's not hotting up.' Neal stood at the foot of the beds. 'So we're going to have to be brave.'

'You're not suggesting a cold shower?' she protested.

'We don't have much choice. Come on: it will only be hell for the first thirty seconds.'

'Maybe the water is running hot in my room.'

'Not a hope. This whole block is served by the same pipes. Out you come.' He whipped back the bedclothes.

'Neal! I don't want a cold shower. You can't force me to have one.'

'No force required...just a little gentle persuasion.'

He pulled her onto her feet, spun her round and pulled her against him, her shoulder blades to his chest. A hand on the back of her head, quite gently he pressed it down and put his teeth to her neck, lightly biting the nape.

Like many other things he had done to her this afternoon, it sent a primitive ripple of pleasure through her. Why the feel of his teeth delicately clenching and unclenching should have this effect she didn't know. But it did and when, at the same time, he started caressing her breasts, her knees went weak.

'This isn't fair,' she muttered.

Neal tipped her head back to rest on his shoulder. 'All's fair in love and war.' He applied his teeth to the lobe of her ear, his hand sliding down her body to the cluster of tawny curls which betrayed that she wasn't a natural ash blonde.

Even to have his hand near the source of her ecstasy made Sarah's defences crumble. How, after living like a nun for so long, she had now, in one afternoon, developed this insatiable need, was a mystery she couldn't rationalise. She only knew that it was so. In silent surrender, she let him walk her to the shower.

Before he turned on the water, Neal turned her to face him. 'It won't be as bad as you imagine,' he murmured, close to her ear.

He was right: it wasn't. For fifteen, perhaps thirty seconds it was like needles of ice, and then the agony was over and it was strangely exhilarating to be under the downpour of water with this man who was now her lover.

Taking a shower with Neal was an erotic game. First he shampooed her hair, the firm massage of his fingers on her scalp followed by a gentler, more sensuous massage of her entire body with handfuls of shower gel. Then she had to lather his body while he was washing his hair. Finally they both rinsed off under another deluge of water which now seemed invigorating rather than freezing.

'Too bad they don't have decent towels. I'd like to wrap you up in a king-size bath sheet, but I'm afraid you'll have to make do with this,' he said, handing her the towel provided.

'What about you?'

'I can dry on a face cloth.'

To her amazement, he could. By the time she was dry, he was too.

Sarah dressed and went back to her room to change her shirt and put on some make-up. At Naomi's insistence she'd had her eyelashes dyed for the trip. She only needed a touch of eye shadow and some lipstick. While she was putting on earrings, she heard voices further down the veranda and then footsteps and a man speaking what sounded like French. As they passed her room a woman answered him. Then the sound of their conversation died away as they headed for the main house.

'We forgot to watch the sunset,' said Neal, stepping into her room after she had responded to his tap on the door. 'We mustn't miss tomorrow's sunrise.'

On the way to the house, she told him about the new-comers. 'Do you speak French?'

'I can get by. Do you?'

'I know the French for e-mail is "mel" from *message électronique* but that's my limit.'

'The chances are they'll speak English,' he said. 'Either way, who needs them? I'm happy talking to you.' He reached for her hand and pressed a kiss into her palm.

After he had bought drinks and carried them to the table where they had lunched, Neal said, 'I'd better take a look at Maureen.'

The painting group were still in their rooms and the French couple were sitting in the well where Neal and Sarah had had coffee. But while he was upstairs, the woman appeared round the corner, a glass of wine in her hand, and came to speak to Sarah.

'Have you been here long?' She spoke English with only a slight accent.

'We arrived this morning...from Kathmandu,' Sarah said. 'Where have you come from?'

'We have been climbing Mera. We were lucky. As we came down the weather changed. I think those going up would not reach the summit.'

A slender woman in her early thirties, she didn't look the rugged type. Her companion, who now came to join her, was older by twenty years with grey hair and a trimmed beard.

'Good evening, *madame*.' He bowed. 'You have eaten here? Is the food good? We are very hungry after climbing a mountain.'

'We've had lunch here. I enjoyed it. I don't think they have the facilities to cook anything elaborate.'

'Whatever it's like, it will be an improvement on the meals prepared by our Sherpa cook,' said the Frenchwoman. 'He was doing his best, but cooking is very difficult in those conditions. I am Maxine and this is Gérard.'

'I'm Sarah.' She sensed they were waiting to be asked to sit down but she wasn't sure if Neal would want that. At that moment, to her relief, he came down the stairs and joined them. Soon after being introduced, he invited the French couple to join them. Whether or not he wished to, courtesy made it unavoidable when the others were clearly eager for conversation.

They turned out to be very good company. Gérard was an executive with one of the biggest supermarket chains in France, but felt he had missed his vocation and should have been a mountaineer.

'I am past the age when a career change is possible,' he said, with a very Gallic shrug, 'but at least I can spend my holidays in the mountains.'

While they were having dinner together, Maxine revealed herself as a computer programmer. Although her job was far more technical than Sarah's, they were working in different areas of the same sphere.

It was a convivial evening but none of them wanted to make a late night of it. Gérard and Maxine had had a long day and were tired. Neal and Sarah had other reasons for wanting to go to bed early.

The French couple left the house first. Neal had already organised transport for himself and Maureen and made the arrangements for the X-ray. They would leave after breakfast and, he hoped, be back before lunch.

Walking back to the annexe, he said, 'Bring what you need for the night to my room.' He ran a hand over his chin. 'I need another shave…don't want to chafe your skin.'

The remark reminded her of the feel of his cheeks against the delicate skin at the tops of her thighs and of the exquisite sensations a little later. But nightfall had brought a sharp drop in the temperature. It was now very cold and the rooms had no heating. Even the most ardent lovers might feel some reluctance to shed their clothes in such conditions. Had she been on her own, she would have been going to bed in her thermals and socks.

She brushed her teeth in her bathroom, then locked up and went next door, knocking before she went in. There was now what appeared to be a double sleeping bag spread on the bed. Looking more closely, she saw that it was actually two single bags opened out and zipped together.

Neal strolled out of the bathroom in the white T-shirt he had been wearing under his shirt at dinner. It emphasised his tanned skin. The short sleeves ended where there was a swell of muscle, not the exaggerated biceps of the iron-pumpers but the gentler and more aesthetically pleasing bulge of an arm exercised in a more natural way.

After she had put down her things, he said, 'Does this feel better?' and caught her wrists in order to place her hands against his newly-shaved cheeks. 'I haven't any aftershave to put on, I'm afraid. It's a luxury I don't have space for on this trip.'

As he dropped his hands, she kept hers where they were, her fingertips on the strongly-marked slant of his cheekbones. 'I like your natural smell. I don't need aftershave to turn me on. You do that by looking at me.'

He gave her a long intent look. 'You 'ave zee same effect on me, *madame*,' he said, in a good imitation of Gérard's accent. Then, in his own voice, 'The bathroom's all yours. I'll be warming the bag for you.'

Taking her hands, he ran his lips over her knuckles. 'Don't be too long. I've been wanting to make love to you for the past couple of hours.'

When she emerged from the bathroom, the room was in darkness apart from a beam of light from a head-torch she had noticed lying on the night table. It was pointed at the far wall so as not to dazzle her.

She had decided there was no point in putting on a

nightdress only to have it whipped off her, and anyway it was only marginally colder without it than with it. She didn't have to stand shivering, wondering how to wriggle her way into the bag, for long. It opened for her. She dived in and a moment later had the additional covering of Neal's warm body lying over hers. He closed the zip. Briefly, there was a draught as he stretched a long arm to switch off the torch. Then they were both cocooned in a dark downy nest which, now she was in it, she wouldn't have changed for a centrally-heated suite in the world's most luxurious hotel.

In the early hours of the morning Neal was woken by his pager. He shut it off, hoping neither the sound nor his movements had disturbed Sarah. But it was soon apparent that she was deeply asleep and unlikely to be woken by the head-torch if he kept its beam low and pointed at the floor.

Quickly and quietly he put on some clothes and his boots. Outside it was very cold but there were no clouds and the sky was brilliant with stars, promising a clear sunrise.

He had given Delia firm instructions to call him at any hour should her sister's condition give her any cause for alarm. But in his experience, the female sex could be classified in one of two broad groups.

There were those who rushed their children to a doctor at the first sign of a sore throat, demanding antibiotics. And there were the others who dealt with all minor ailments themselves and even when seriously ill shrank from 'being a nuisance'. Delia and Maureen belonged to the second category.

Walking on the grass, he went round the house to look up at their bedroom window. There was no light showing. Satisfied that they were having a peaceful night, he returned to his own bed.

For a while he lay awake, warming his cold hands by tucking them under his armpits, thinking about the woman asleep beside him. In terms of factual information, he knew more about Gérard and Maxine than he did about Sarah.

Not that the verbal CVs that people gave out about themselves were as important or revealing as their unconscious messages.

Simply by being with her, he knew a lot about Sarah's character and her instincts. Especially her instincts, he thought, smiling to himself.

Each time they made love she was increasingly generous in giving pleasure as well as receiving it. He had never known anyone more passionate or more imaginative. The promise of her lovely mouth, first noticed on the plane, had already been amply fulfilled.

Another thing he had learned about her since they came here was that she had given birth. It left signs on a woman's body that might not be recognisable to a layman but any doctor would recognise at once.

Why it was something she didn't speak of he could only guess. Perhaps the child had been stillborn or had died later. Whatever, it was clearly something she didn't wish to confide to him.

His hands warm, he turned on his side, sliding one under the pillow and putting his other arm round her while shifting his body closer.

The smooth silky warmth of her back against his chest and lower body made him feel wider awake than the sharp air in the garden. His hand wandered over her belly and up to the softness of her breasts. He was tempted to wake her with a caress he knew she liked. Then he decided she needed her sleep and it would be better to wait until morning.

Their time together was short, but not that short.

*　　*　　*

Next day, after watching the sunrise over the Himalaya, they went back to bed and made love before breakfast.

Later, learning that Sarah would be on her own that morning, Maxine invited her to join them on a walk to a lookout tower on the summit of the Nagarkot ridge. Sarah was feeling lazy after what, by her standards, had been an unprecedented debauch, but she felt the walk would restore her energies more effectively than relaxing at the farm and perhaps being bothered by Roger.

Neal and the sisters were already back when the walkers returned. One of the painters told Sarah that Delia was putting Maureen to bed and Neal had gone to his room.

Following him there, Sarah found him writing postcards.

'Did the X-ray confirm your diagnosis?' she asked, after they had kissed.

He nodded. 'She'll need a lot of rest until her lungs are clear. At her age pneumonia can really knock the stuffing out of people. Whether she'll be fit to fly back with the others is a bit doubtful. Maybe we can pull strings and get her upgraded to first class. That takes a lot of the aggro out of a long flight. How was your morning?'

'Energetic! They set a cracking pace.'

'In that case I advise that you take it easy this afternoon. Bed rest and lots of mouth-to-mouth resuscitation.'

His teasing lit a warm glow inside her. It was then she knew she had fallen irreversibly in love with him.

That evening the sunset matched the sunrise in its beauty and grandeur.

To see five of the world's ten highest peaks among many other mountain tops was, on its own, one of life's major experiences, thought Sarah, as she got ready for dinner. To have recognised love for what it was made the day even more unforgettable.

Again they shared a table with the French couple. With

Gérard present the conversation never strayed far from mountains and climbing. His hero was Anatoli Boukreev, the famous Russian mountaineer who had died in an avalanche on Annapurna after a Christmas Day avalanche.

Neal and Maxine were equally admiring of the Russian's achievements and explained them to Sarah.

'Instead of becoming weaker at high altitudes, as most people do,' said Neal, 'Boukreev seemed to get stronger. They called him "a lung with legs".'

'But, however good they are, not many top-class climbers survive to old age,' said Gérard. 'Boukreev was only thirty-nine, a year older than your compatriot Kennedy. He also was a king among climbers.'

They had not exchanged surnames. He was unaware that the man he spoke of bore the same last name as Neal.

'I don't like to think about death...all those frozen bodies out there on the mountains for ever,' said Maxine, with a shiver. 'Let's talk about something more cheerful. While you were in Kathmandu, did you see any of the embroidery they call "crewel", Sarah? I'd like to buy some for curtains.'

'Women! They can never go anywhere without wanting to shop,' Gérard said, with a theatrical groan.

They all laughed. Only Sarah was aware that Neal, although he had spoken freely of Boukreev, had let down some kind of internal blind when the English climber was mentioned. His eyes, usually bright with interest or humour, had all at once gone strangely blank.

CHAPTER SIX

THEIR French friends were leaving next day. When they had said goodnight to them and were alone in Neal's room, he said, 'You may have had enough of being here, but if you can bear it I'd like to hang on for another twenty-four hours to make sure Maureen is responding to the medication I've given her.'

'I'm happy to stay for as long as you like,' she said, smiling. 'I like it...despite the cold showers. There's more to life than hot water and gourmet food.'

He put his arms round her. 'Such as?'

She slid her arms round his neck. 'Such as this...and that—' with a look indicating the sleeping bags. 'I wonder what the cleaning people thought about the beds being pushed together?'

'I should think it happens all the time, at least when the rooms are being used by people of opposite sexes.'

'If we're going to stay a bit, wouldn't it make sense to cancel the other room and share this one?'

'OK, I'll do that tomorrow.'

'I don't understand why you booked two rooms?'

'In case you changed your mind at the last moment and there wasn't another room free. Somehow I had the feeling that you weren't too sure about this situation.'

'No, I wasn't. But I am now. It was a good decision. I'm enjoying it.'

'I hoped you would.'

Sarah laughed. 'You never had the smallest doubt of it, you cocksure beast.'

As Neal raised an eyebrow she recognised the unintentional *double entendre* and couldn't help blushing, even though she knew he was only pretending to be shocked.

He chuckled and hugged her close. 'You've led a sheltered life, Sarah. Most of the women journalists I come across say things that would curl your hair. They curl mine sometimes.'

Until that moment she hadn't consciously realised that he never used the words she hated hearing from Matthew. Not that she ever made a fuss about it. Her own puritanical upbringing had made her, perhaps, too easy-going with her son. She had hoped, was still hoping, he would grow out of the phase of wanting to shock his elders. But he hadn't so far.

Her cheek against Neal's chest, she thought how great it would be if she could confide her problems and ask his advice. But that wasn't on the agenda. This relationship they were having was strictly short-term, strictly for laughs.

After a moment, she said, 'Anyway you were quite right. You're a terrific lover. I can't speak from wide experience, but I've never had such a great time in bed.' She lifted her face. 'Isn't it time we were in bed?'

'High time!'

During the night she woke up and found him missing. Had he gone to the bathroom?

When, some minutes later, it was the room door that opened, it gave her a momentary fright until she realised it was Neal coming in, not an intruder.

'Where have you been?' she asked in an undertone, fearing a normal voice might disturb their neighbours.

'Just checking.'

Once back inside the bags, he explained more fully. 'The early hours of the morning are the time when sick people tend to wake up. Sometimes they get in a panic and need reassuring.'

'Maureen has Delia to calm her.'

'Delia might get worried too, but not like to wake me. Anyway they're both fast asleep. What woke you up?'

'I don't know. Some night noise maybe. You must be freezing. Let me warm you.'

'It's only my hands that are cold.'

'Put them here.' She seized them and tucked them between her thighs, stifling a gasp as his chilled fingers met her warm flesh.

'Mm…that feels wonderful. Where can I put my cold nose?'

'Here.' She put her arms round him and drew his head down to her breasts.

For a little while Neal let her warm him, but soon his hands started to move and his lips to search the soft curves where his head had been pillowed. With a sigh of pleasure she surrendered her body to his caresses, secure in the knowledge that, with him, she wouldn't be left in the air when, his own needs satisfied, he went back to sleep.

Each time they made love she reached fever-pitch more quickly. Soon she had to grab the pillow and pull it over her face to smother the moans he forced from her. Her spine arched, she spread her legs, lost in that private place where the mind cut out, leaving only the senses in a whirl of rapturous sensations.

Time and again he drove her close to the brink but then stopped her and made her rest, tantalised almost beyond endurance, yet knowing, because he had shown her before, that every pause would intensify the final starburst of ecstasy.

When it was over, when she was momentarily spent, only then did he take her with a fierce driving force that quickly re-energised her with a need to drive him to the same brink and beyond.

The beds shuddered, jolted and creaked as their bodies lunged back and forth in the primeval ritual of mating. At the end, as she felt him convulse, Sarah experienced a piercing sense of loss because there could never be any logical outcome to their loving. This was all they could ever share, a few nights of glorious but ultimately sterile passion.

To her dismay she felt her eyes fill with tears her eyelids could not contain. They trailed down her cheeks and Neal, who was pressing soft kisses all over her face in a silent expression of thanks, felt their moisture with his cheeks.

But instead of withdrawing, repelled, as she feared he might, he became even more tender.

'I'm sorry...I don't usually do this,' she said, in a shaky whisper.

'Perhaps you should,' he said softly. 'It does women good to cry.'

'When they have something to cry about. I haven't. I'm very happy.'

'Maybe that's why. I get the feeling you haven't had enough of it.'

'I expect I've had as much as most people. I don't suppose your life has been all roses.' She was remembering his reaction to Gérard's remark at dinner.

'My life has been OK. Some of the people I care for haven't had it so good.'

He shifted his body from hers, switched on the headtorch and gave her a tissue from the pack on the table. 'I'm going away for a minute. I'll be right back.'

In his absence, Sarah mopped her eyes. He had been very sweet about her burst of emotion but she must take care not to let it happen again. Men didn't like tearful women and by nature she wasn't a weeper...except very occasionally, in private, when life was being more than usually difficult.

He came back. 'Would you like some water?'

'Yes, please.' She sat up, trying not to shiver in the cold air outside the bags.

'Put this round you, honey.' Neal fetched his fleece and wrapped it round her like a shawl.

'What about you?'

'I'm tougher than you are.' He opened the bottle of water he kept on the night table, filled two glasses brought from the bathroom and handed one of them to her.

Sarah drank the water quickly and snuggled down again. When Neal joined her she was lying on her back. He turned her onto her side and arranged himself close behind her, his hand on her hip.

'Go to sleep now. Goodnight.'

'Goodnight,' she echoed.

As far as she could tell, he was asleep within minutes. But she didn't want to sleep yet. She wanted to savour the primitive pleasure of being a female under the protection of a strong and resourceful male. Even as a child—least of all as a child—she had never known what it was to feel safe from everything bad. She did now. But it wasn't going to last long. While it lasted she wanted to fix it in her mind: to remember when it was over and she had only herself to rely on.

Next morning they went for a walk. The tracks in the region surrounding the farm weren't easy-walking. Every downhill stretch was followed by a steep incline. There were very few level areas.

'You set the pace. Take it easy. We don't need to go far. I don't want you to get back exhausted,' said Neal, as they set out.

Before leaving, he had spent some time with Maureen and was satisfied that her medication was working.

They walked for about an hour, then stopped for a rest which Sarah knew was more for her benefit than his. He had walked this kind of terrain many times and was in fine shape. Her life was mainly sedentary and, although she had done some fitness-training for the trip, she would need to train hard for months to be capable of keeping up with Neal moving at his natural pace.

He had a small pack with him containing a bottle of water and a bar of chocolate. The place where they were sitting had a fine view of the distant mountain tops.

Presently, glancing at him after a longer than usual pause in their conversation, Sarah sensed that he was thinking of whatever it was that had upset him at dinner the night before.

'Neal...tell me to mind my own business if it's something you don't want to talk about, but the climber called Kennedy that Gérard mentioned last night...was he a member of your family?'

'He was my elder brother.'

There was another pause, making her feel he was going to leave it at that.

Embarrassed, regretting her intrusion, she was surprised when he went on, 'I love my parents and my sisters but Chris was special...my hero...my closest friend. He left a massive hole in all our lives. We still can't get used to the idea that he's gone...forever.'

She knew the feeling, but she didn't say so. It wouldn't help him to know she had been through it too.

'Was it another avalanche?'

'No...a careless mistake that he ought not to have made...wouldn't have made if his mind had been focused. But his personal life had gone wrong. What happened was most likely the result of thinking about that when he should have been concentrating on what he was doing.'

They were sitting on a rocky outcrop, Neal with his arms round his knees, one lean brown hand clasping his other wrist. The stainless steel strap of his watch winked in the sunlight.

'Chris fell for a girl who knew the kind of man he was and pretended she could cope with that,' he continued. 'She couldn't. She tried to change him into the sort of husband she wanted. In the end the marriage broke down. Chris had inherited a lot of money from his godfather who had no one else to leave it to. Some shyster lawyer helped Cleo take Chris to the cleaners. He didn't care about the money. It was facing the truth about Cleo that got to him.'

'How did they ever get together if they were so different?' Sarah asked.

'It was the usual story...infatuation versus common sense with infatuation winning,' Neal said cynically. 'She was beautiful and very sexy and Chris spent most of his time in the company of climbers in a largely male environment. He was completely bowled over.'

And if he was anything like you, so was she, I expect, thought Sarah.

'Were you alike...you and your brother?' she asked.

'He was much better-looking. They made a spectacular couple. Most of the nationals sent photographers to the church. Chances are Cleo invited them. She liked being the centre of attention. She did look wonderful on her wedding day,' Neal conceded. 'But her looks were strictly skin-deep. Under the surface she was a self-centred bitch.'

'I wonder why she wanted him? Presumably she didn't know he was rich until after they were married.'

'A lot of women wanted Chris. Apart from his looks, he was an outstanding climber and a thoroughly nice guy. He could have married any number of girls who would have been happy to stay behind while he climbed, or maybe to set up home somewhere near the mountain he was tackling. He picked out the one who wasn't. We all tried to make him see sense. But he was insanely in love. From what I've seen of it, love is a form of insanity.'

'Not always,' Sarah said quietly.

'No, not always. My parents are still together and my sisters' marriages are working. But a helluva lot of our generation's relationships end the same way Chris's did.'

He had been staring at the mountains, his strong profile

etched by the bright light. Now he turned and gave her a long interrogative look.

She knew he was curious about her, but she didn't want to unpack all the emotional baggage she kept in a locked boxroom at the back of her mind.

If this time with him were going to continue in real life, then she would have bared her soul to him. As things stood, was there any point?

She said, 'My mother's a widow. I was the only child of two only children, so I don't have any relations.'

'Are you close to your mother?'

'Yes.' It was true in one sense. Her mother was her dependant and always would be. But they had nothing in common except painful memories.

She looked at her watch. The meals at the farm were served at fixed times. 'Ought we to be getting back?'

'If you like.' Neal rose, offering a hand to pull her to her feet.

Even that casual contact sent a current of excitement through her. All the time she was with him, her senses were in a permanent state of semi-arousal.

He must feel the same, she thought, as he let go her hand only to sweep an arm round her and kiss her hard on the mouth. There was anger as well as desire in that fierce fusion of lips.

Afterwards, walking back, she felt that he'd wanted to take her then and there and, had they been anywhere else, would have done so. But here in Nepal the landscape wasn't conducive to al fresco love-making and also such conduct would be shocking to any Nepalese who happened to see it. Not, from what she had read, that they were an inhibited race. Bhotia women, living in the highest regions near the Tibetan border, sometimes had several husbands, usually brothers. But in their public behaviour the Nepalese were more modest and circumspect than Westerners.

*   *   *

Neal was annoyed with himself. He recognised the punitive element in the way he had kissed Sarah and he wasn't used to feeling irrational emotions and didn't like it.

Nor did he understand why he had told her about Chris. It would have been easy enough to deflect her curiosity.

It was a long time since his brother's death and gradually the sense of loss had abated, at least for himself and his sisters. For his parents it was a different and deeper pain. They had had loving bonds with each of their children and had been equally proud of their different achievements. Being a united family had made everyone's grief a bit more bearable than it would otherwise have been.

Inevitably, being near mountains made him think of Chris more than he did when he was in London, but why he had felt impelled to tell Sarah about him, and about Cleo, was something he didn't understand.

Also it irked him that, having confided in her, she hadn't trusted him with more than the most basic information about her family background.

Her 'yes' in reply to his question about her closeness to her mother had been close to a snub.

She was willing to permit the closest physical intimacies, but her past and most of her present life, apart from the here and now, was off limits.

He wasn't accustomed to not being trusted by women. As a doctor, he was used to having them feel especially at ease with him, sometimes confiding more than he wished to hear. The barrier raised by Sarah was a new experience. He didn't like the suspicion that she might be merely using him, the way men often used women, purely for sexual enjoyment.

He had never done that. He had always felt more than lust for the women in his life, although never anything approaching the consuming passion which had destroyed his brother.

In Neal's view the West had a lot to learn from people

like the Nepalese. Traditionally, their marriages were rooted in practical considerations. Now, in some areas, outside influences were changing that. Love matches were gaining ground and, very often, leading to the same unhappiness that afflicted more sophisticated cultures.

When—if—he married, it would be based on the solid foundation of friendship. As it happened, his attitude to marriage was undergoing a change, probably as a result of meeting Gérard and Maxine. Clearly they had a rock-solid partnership founded on their mutual passion for mountains. Talking to them had made him realise that having a permanent travelling companion must be good... better, in some ways, than being independent.

Sarah sat in the back of the taxi with Maureen and Delia, feeling relieved that they were leaving Nagarkot. She and Neal were being dropped off at Bhaktapur while the others went on to spend the rest of their visit in a comfortable hotel in Kathmandu.

Why she was glad to depart from a place where she had been happy was difficult to pin down. Outwardly nothing had changed, but inwardly she felt something *had* changed. Neal was not as open and relaxed as he had been at the beginning of their time there.

Was she beginning to bore him? she asked herself, looking at the back of his head as the car jolted downhill.

She and the two older women were sharing the back seat with Neal in front, talking to the driver. They were sharing a joke about something and, as Neal turned his head to grin at the smaller man, the angle of his cheekbone and the vertical crease that appeared when he was extremely amused sent a little shiver of wanting through her.

They had made love last night and again before breakfast. On that score everything was fine between them. His appetite for her showed no sign of abating. He was beginning to convince her that she was as desirable as he told her she was.

It was on some other level that she couldn't define that their relationship had changed. Could it possibly be that he sensed she had fallen for him and was concerned that, when the time came to say goodbye, she wouldn't accept that what they had shared had just been a holiday romance to which there would be no sequel?

'I must confess I am *longing* for a long hot bath,' said Delia. 'The farm was delightful but a little short on creature comforts. You young things don't mind that, but at our age beds and baths and food become increasingly important.'

The two men still being engrossed in their conversation, Sarah said, 'I'm not that young, Delia. I can't wait to wallow in warm water.'

Maureen, who was sitting between them, patted her arm. 'You look gloriously young to us. How I should love to be your age again. It's such a bore getting old.'

'Being young isn't much fun either,' said her sister. 'One is so unsure of oneself, and falling in and out of love can be agony. Looking back, I didn't enjoy my twenties much. I'd say between thirty and the menopause are a woman's best years.'

'Hear, hear,' Maureen agreed. She turned to Sarah. 'You're in those "best years", my dear. Make the most of them.'

Sarah guessed they were intrigued by her relationship with Neal but would consider it bad form to indulge their curiosity. For her part she couldn't help wondering if they had ever experienced the wild bouts of sensual abandon she had had since arriving at Nagarkot. It was hard to guess what people were or had once been like in those private areas of their lives. At least now she wouldn't grow old without knowing what ecstasy was.

But perhaps, if you could only have it for a short time,

it was better not to know, she thought wryly. There was that old saying 'What you never have, you never miss'. If she hadn't met Neal, she wouldn't have known how passionately she could respond to an ardent lover. She would have gone on subsisting on daydreams and fantasies, an unsatisfying substitute for the real thing, but better than nothing. Better than spending the rest of her life remembering this all too brief idyll.

No, she admonished herself. No, that was negative thinking. Any experience of love must always be better than missing it altogether.

By mid-morning she and Neal were having coffee on the terrace of a café in the ancient city's main square and the others were continuing their journey to Kathmandu.

'Come on, let's go and pay our respects to King Bhupatrindra Malla,' said Neal, when their cups were empty.

He paid the bill, then took Sarah's hand and led her across the large square where tourists were outnumbered by local people, the women wearing distinctive saris of finely-woven black wool with scarlet borders, pleated in front and raised at the back to show off the patterns tattooed on their calves.

The statue of one of the city's kings was perched on top of a pillar facing the most elaborate and beautiful gateway she had ever seen.

'It's one of the wonders of the world, but not many people bother to come and see it,' said Neal. 'All that gold tells you how fabulously rich the Malla kings were. We'll go through and look at the kings' bathing pool.'

She was grateful to him for taking the trouble to show her a place he had probably seen many times before. Inside the golden gate they were intercepted by a Gurkha soldier who insisted that Sarah should take a photograph of Neal and himself. Sarah was glad of the opportunity to snap Neal. She was eager to have some mementoes of their time together but sensed that he wouldn't want to pose for snapshots, and it was difficult to take good ones when he was unaware of her doing it.

Compared with the sturdy little soldier, who seemed to feel it was his duty to oblige snap-happy foreigners even to the extent of flourishing his kukri, Neal looked very tall and lithe. Quickly, she took two shots in case one didn't come out.

They had lunch on the roof of a guest-house where four American tourists asked Neal if he would take a picture of them. He obliged them with the easy charm that made people open up to him and must be an important asset in his work as a journalist, thought Sarah, watching him chatting to them.

When he rejoined her, he said, 'We could stay here overnight, but the lodgings are fairly basic and I heard what you and Delia were saying about hot baths so we'll make tracks for something a bit more de luxe...and from now on you're my guest. No arguments, please.'

It was said in a tone of authority that would have raised some women's hackles. Sarah wasn't sure she was comfortable about staying somewhere luxurious at his expense. But she could see that he was determined and perhaps it was ungracious to deny him the generous gesture. She had no idea what columnists on national newspapers earned, but it was probably astronomical compared with her income.

'It's very kind of you, Neal.'

'I'm being selfish, not kind,' he said dryly. 'A double sleeping bag has its uses, but it's limiting. There are things I want to do with you that weren't possible at Nargakot.'

A few hours later, he showed her what he meant.

As Sarah's time ran out, the Everest Marathon organisers, observers and runners were starting to assemble at another of the city's hotels.

Most afternoons, Neal would take Sarah over there and introduce her to people who would be his companions when she had gone. Several of them were doctors studying the effects of high altitude on various parts of the human body.

Among the runners was an attractive female Army officer. Sarah couldn't help feeling a twinge of jealousy, an emotion she had always despised and disliked recognising in herself.

The hotel where the runners were staying was an old Rana palace, not as comfortable inside as the Yak and Yeti, but with a romantic façade and a large lawn in front where tea and drinks were served in an atmosphere redolent of gracious eras long gone.

Sometimes, in the evening, she and Neal would go out for a meal with some of the other medical people. As the wine and beer flowed, anecdotes and jokes from their training days would surface, some of them nearer the knuckle than Sarah was used to but witty enough to be acceptable. Once, when one of the other men started telling a story, Neal stopped him. It was lightly and tactfully done, without putting a damper on the proceedings, and Sarah was grateful to him for sparing her blushes. It gave her a very warm feeling to know that he felt so protective towards her.

But, increasingly, as the days passed, her happiness was overshadowed by the imminence of their parting.

For Neal, when they said goodbye, there would be the excitement and camaraderie of the pre-Marathon trek to fall back on. For her there was only the flight home and a return to a life which, from her new perspective, seemed even duller and more limited than it had before.

On the afternoon of her last day, she went to the hotel

where her own trekking group were staying to check that there was no change in the departure arrangements.

To her surprise, Sandy's manner was much more friendly than it had been at the outset.

She went as far as to say, 'You made the right decision. I've never met a worse bunch of moaners than this lot. What have you been up to?'

Sarah mentioned a few of the things she had done in their absence, wondering what Sandy would say if told that a lot of her time had been spent in the arms of a man who, two weeks ago, she hadn't known existed.

'Are you going to have dinner with us tonight?' the trek guide asked.

'I've arranged to eat with some friends I've made.'

'OK. See you at the airport.'

As it turned out, Neal had arranged for them to dine alone. But at no time during the meal did he mention meeting again when they were both back at home. He would not be back for a month, so perhaps it wasn't surprising that he wasn't thinking ahead.

That night he made love to her with a tenderness that was almost unbearably moving.

'I wish you could come with us,' he said softly, close to her ear as they lay locked together afterwards. 'I'm sure you'd enjoy it.'

'I wish I could too,' she murmured, knowing this might be the last time she would ever experience this special private moment. She would never be able to do this with anyone else. Her heart and her body were his, now and for ever.

In the morning, he woke her with kisses, but there wasn't time to make love again. Her flight took off at nine and, according to Sandy, there was a lot of red tape to get through at the airport.

Room Service brought them an early breakfast. Sarah

had had a quick shower. Her knapsack was packed. She drank two cups of tea, but didn't feel like eating.

'You ought to have something inside you,' said Neal.

'I'll have something on the plane.' Inside, she was bracing herself for their final moments together. Whatever it cost her, she must try not to let him see how painful their parting would be for her.

In the taxi, Neal exchanged some remarks with the driver. Halfway there, he reached for her hand and squeezed it. The gesture was nearly Sarah's undoing. She had a lump in her throat and an ache in her chest, but she was determined not to show her emotions, except for answering the pressure of his fingers with hers.

Outside the terminal building, the usual horde of men and boys descended on the taxi, hoping for luggage to carry. Having told the driver to wait for him, Neal shepherded her through the pestering press and into the relative peace of the terminal.

'Don't wait, Neal. I'll find the others. There's no need to hang about,' she said, trying to sound cheerful.

'I nearly forgot.' He unzipped one of the pockets on the legs of his trousers and produced a folded piece of pale yellow silk.

Shaking it out, he lifted it over her head and drew it round her neck: the traditional farewell offering to departing travellers.

Holding it by both ends, he looked down into her eyes, his own expression unreadable.

'Take care, Sarah. Goodbye...and thank you.' He bent to kiss her cheek. Then he let go of the scarf and did what she had asked, turning away and striding out of the building.

CHAPTER SEVEN

BETWEEN touching down at Gatwick and boarding the
train that would take her to her home town, Sarah had an
hour to wait at the rail station. She rang Naomi to ask if
everything had gone smoothly in her absence.

'Yes, but I've missed you terribly. Have you had a great
time?'

'Wonderful.'

'I'll be at the station to meet you. What time are you
due in?'

Three hours later they were exchanging a bear hug.

'Are you half-dead with jet lag?' Naomi asked, as they
drew apart. 'You don't look it. You look terrific...never
seen you looking better. Globe-trotting obviously suits
you. Was the trek tougher or less tough than you expected?'

'I didn't go on the trek. The others were all much older.
I backed out of it.'

Naomi looked startled. 'So what did you do? Were you
comfortable going it alone?'

Sarah had already given a lot of thought to telling or
not telling Naomi what had happened to her. She had decided she couldn't keep it to herself. She needed to talk
to someone and knew she could rely on her friend not to
betray her confidences.

'I wasn't alone,' she said, as they left the station building. 'I did what you told me to do. A gorgeous man ma-
terialised and instead of backing off I fell into his arms.'

'You're kidding me!' Naomi exclaimed. Then, as Sarah
shook her head, she added, 'I can hardly believe it. You've
had such a lousy love life. Sometimes I've felt your luck

was never going to change. What's he like? Where did you meet him?'

'We met on the plane going out. He's still in Nepal. He's involved in the Everest Marathon...not as a runner. He's a journalist.' She had already decided not to mention Neal's other profession.

'When is he coming back? Where does he live?'

'In London...but I shan't be seeing him again.'

'Why not?'

'It isn't an ongoing thing. It was lovely while it lasted, but it doesn't have a future.'

'Why not?' her friend repeated. 'Oh, God, don't tell me he's married?'

'If he had been, it wouldn't have happened.'

'They don't always tell you,' Naomi said dryly. A long time ago, she herself had had an unwitting and painful entanglement with a married man. It had left her extremely cynical about the male sex's capacity for duplicity.

'He definitely isn't married,' Sarah assured her. 'He's anti-marriage. His brother had a bad marriage and it's put Neal off going that route. He has no need for a wife. He's a ten-out-of-ten with all the perks that go with it.'

'Genuine ten-out-of-tens have brains as well as sex appeal,' said Naomi. 'They don't want to play the field for the rest of their lives. They're looking for one special woman. What makes you think you can't be his special person?'

They had arrived at her car. She was on the driver's side, Sarah had gone to the passenger door. Looking across the top of the car, she said, 'He's thirty-six.'

'So?'

'Oh, come on...you know how old I am.'

'Does he?'

'He didn't ask and I didn't tell him. His guess may be a year or two under, but he'd have to be short of some marbles not to know that I've been around longer than he has.'

Naomi unlocked, got in and reached across to unlock the door for Sarah. When they were both in the car, she said, 'Men marry younger women all the time. Why should it make any difference the other way round?'

'Because it does, and you know it. A man of my age and a woman of his can marry or set up as partners and no one thinks anything of it. That's the normal age gap. When the woman is older it isn't. It's the subject of endless gossip and speculation.'

'I wouldn't let *that* bother me,' Naomi said, turning to face her. 'What other people think doesn't matter a damn. It's whether the people involved in a relationship are comfortable with it that counts. This decision to end the affair, is that your idea?'

'It was mutual. When we said goodbye at the airport, he didn't suggest meeting again and neither did I. We both knew it wouldn't translate into real life.'

'But he does have your address or your telephone number in case he changes his mind about that?'

'Not my exact address. He knows where I live. He's a journalist. He could trace me from that…if he wanted to. But he won't. I've thought about it a lot and I reckon I'm lucky to have had such a wonderful time with him. It was literally out of this world and should stay that way. In real life we have almost nothing in common. To try to prolong it wouldn't work.'

'If you didn't have much in common, how come you got on so well?' Naomi asked.

Sarah hesitated. 'We spent a lot of time in bed. He was a marvellous lover. But that's not a basis for a lasting relationship.'

'Maybe not, but it's a good start, bed being where lots of relationships seem to go wrong.' Naomi switched on the ignition. 'And if he's switched on your libido, that's a genie it isn't easy to put back in the bottle.'

'Maybe not, but at least now I *know* what I'm missing. That's better than going to my grave never knowing what all the fuss was about.'

'The hole in that argument being that, with any luck, you won't be going to your grave for thirty or forty years. That's a helluva long time to live on a memory,' said her friend. 'Tell me some more about him.'

'I'll show you a photograph as soon as I've had my films developed. Did you get my postcard?'

'Not yet. How long had you known him before he lured you into bed?'

'A few days. I did resist him for a bit. Now it seems like some crazy dream…something I read, not something that really happened.'

'It happened,' was Naomi's comment. 'I should have known what it was the minute I saw you. Great sex gives women a glow like nothing else, not even an orgy of shopping. When I had that whirl with Philip six years ago people kept asking what I'd been doing to myself.' She gave a yelp of amusement. 'It was what *he* was doing that was making the difference.'

'Mm, I remember,' said Sarah, thinking back to the time of Naomi's longest and happiest liaison. But it hadn't lasted. Philip had wanted too many concessions in his favour without being ready to make any himself.

'Will you tell your mother you didn't do the trek?' asked Naomi.

'I'll have to, but I shan't tell her about Neal. Apart from the fact that she'd be horrified by the moral aspect, it would only worry and unsettle her. I'm her security. She couldn't cope on her own and she's frightened of being deserted.'

'She's a selfish old woman,' Naomi said bluntly. 'She battens on you, Sarah. They both do. Matthew's even worse than she is. Mrs A is old and disabled. He's young and strong. He should be standing on his own feet, not bringing home his dirty laundry and expecting you to wait on him.'

'If it hadn't been for Mum, I wouldn't have gone to Nepal and had my adventure,' said Sarah.

Naomi snorted. She had never soft-pedalled her opinions of Sarah's mother and son. More than once they had come perilously close to a stand-up knock-down fight when Naomi had expressed what she considered useful home truths but which had been seen by Sarah as incursions beyond the boundaries of friendly advice.

'It's the only useful thing she's ever done for you,' Naomi said bluntly. 'I'd hoped the trip would give you a new perspective on your domestic problems. It's way past the time when you broke out...lived for yourself for a change.'

'That's what I've just been doing.'

'For two measly weeks...big deal! You need to break out and stay out. Not step back inside the cage and lock the door on yourself until the unlikely event that your mother wins another competition in your name.'

'Why are you snarling at me?'

'I'm snarling because I'm envious,' Naomi said crossly. 'Don't you see? What's happened to you is a dream come true. Millions of women like us—single mothers on the wrong side of forty—imagine that very thing: a wonderful man looming up out of nowhere and whipping us into bed and maybe, just maybe, into the kind of future we've always yearned for. No, hear me out...' she said as Sarah started to speak.

Just then they stopped at some traffic lights. Naomi yanked on the hand brake and turned to face her.

'For most of us, it's never going to happen. It's a pipe dream...we know that. You're the rare special case. To you it actually *has* happened. But instead of thanking your stars and damn well making the most of it, you've decided to chicken out when the thing's only halfway through. Is it any wonder I'm snarling? If I were in your shoes I'd be following through.'

'There's nothing to follow through. We're like people from different planets who happened to meet somewhere in outer space. Take away the physical attraction and there's nothing left.'

'I don't believe that,' said Naomi. 'You wouldn't jump into bed with someone you didn't like. What's all this about different planets? Oh, he's from Mars and you're from Venus. There's always that to contend with, even with the boy next door. So what are the other big snags...apart from the age gap?'

Sarah had foreseen that Naomi might not see the affair from the same perspective that she did, but she hadn't bargained for being pressured so early or with such vehemence.

'He's from a different background. Better off...better educated...better—'

'Is he a snob?' Naomi interrupted.

'No, not at all.'

'Then why are you being an inverted snob?'

'I'm not. I'm just facing facts. People *aren't* all the same. My father was a policeman who, if he hadn't dropped dead, would have been charged with beating up suspects. Neal's parents—'

Again, her friend cut her short. 'You're not responsible for your dad's misdemeanours. You were one of his victims, for God's sake. Most families have some skeletons in their closets. If you have any sense, when Neal is due back in England, you'll drop him a friendly note so that he knows where to find you and let him take it from there. Is he a freelance journalist?'

'No, he works for one of the nationals.'

'Then contact him via his paper. Send him an

e-mail…say what a great time you had…ask if he'd like some prints of your holiday snaps. What have you got to lose? The worst he can do is ignore you.'

In Nepal, where it was early evening, Neal was having a pre-dinner drink with a group of other people involved in the marathon. Among them, in the chair next to his, was the Army medical officer.

She was attractive and friendly. As a colleague he found her good value. As a woman she left him cold.

He found himself missing Sarah. At the same time he knew it had been sensible to allow a cooling-off period, to hold back from any commitment to see each other again.

She had obviously felt the same way. Her manner when they said goodbye had been composed. He had thought she might be upset but, if she had felt any emotion, it had been under control.

Wondering what she was doing, he wished he knew more about her background and had a clearer impression of her home life.

Last night, while she was airborne, he had missed having her close to him in bed. It had seemed strange to wake up and find himself alone. Tonight it would be the same. But in the morning they would be on the move. Tomorrow night he'd be sharing a tent with another member of the medical team. Before the end of the week he'd be back to normal, back to being on his own, part of a group but not one half of a pair.

It could be that, in a month's time when he hit the UK, he wouldn't want to pick up the threads of their relationship. She might feel the same way. They might both have reached the conclusion that what they'd shared here had been good, but not so good that they wanted to pursue it.

It was one of those 'only time would tell' situations.

Right now he felt strangely bereft, as if some important component of his life had gone missing.

It was a natural reaction. She had been a lovely woman: great company in and out of bed, as different from Cleo, his brother's widow, as if they were different species.

But that didn't alter the fact that before he met Sarah he'd been content with his life. And most likely would be again, once he'd had time to adjust.

In the early hours of the morning, when she had been home for a week and still wasn't sleeping properly, Sarah got up and went to her office, formerly Matthew's bedroom.

Now, when he was at home, he slept in the loft conversion reached by a pull-down ladder. Before Sarah had had all her working equipment in her bedroom where there hadn't been adequate room for it.

In warm pyjamas and a wool dressing gown, she sat down at her computer. Roving the World Wide Web on the Internet might distract her from the thoughts which were turning her into an insomniac.

Sometimes these middle-of-the-night excursions took her to places it would have been wiser to avoid. Once she had found her way to the website run by the clinic where she had discovered that Neal was a doctor. Another time she had been to the on-line department of Pilgrims Book House in whose real-world garden restaurant Rose had collapsed.

One night she had been unable to resist the temptation to search cyberspace for news of the Everest Marathon. But all she had found was a report of another mountain marathon, nothing to do with the one she was interested in.

Tonight, after checking out a couple of websites recommended in a magazine someone had lent her mother, she gave in to an impulse to search for information about Chris Kennedy, Neal's dead brother.

Within seconds of typing his name, she had half a dozen leads. She followed them, one by one, until when she clicked on one link a photograph began to appear.

It was slow to load. At first all she could see was a horizontal band of background: a mountain. Then the top of a dark head appeared, the hairline so like Neal's that she felt her heart give a lurch. The rest of the forehead appeared, followed by a pair of dark eyebrows. But the eyes beneath them were not the amused grey eyes she remembered. Chris, when she saw his whole face, was recognisably Neal's brother but not, in her view, better-looking as Neal had claimed.

She spent a long time trying to analyse what Chris's face lacked that made Neal so much more attractive...at least to her.

When she had shown the snapshot of Neal with the Gurkha soldier to Naomi, it had prompted another lecture of the foolishness of letting him slip out of her life without some attempt to recapture and hold his interest.

There were moments when Sarah tried to convince herself that Naomi was right. But in her heart she knew it was wishful thinking. If she had been on her own, it might have been different. She could have transplanted herself to London. But even if her mother could be persuaded to move, there was no way Neal would want to involve himself with an elderly woman in poor health.

Then there was Matthew to consider. When she thought about Neal and Matthew confronting each other, she knew the whole idea was impossible. Even Naomi had conceded there was a problem there. Matthew had never known his father. His grandfather had died when he was six. He had grown up without any male influence other than that of his teachers. He wouldn't take kindly to a stranger supplanting him in his mother's affections.

*   *   *

Knowing the date when Neal was due back, Sarah couldn't help wondering if he *would* track her down and call her.

A week passed and no call came. It might be that he was too busy with matters to do with his job to have time for any private detective work, she told herself.

Then, one evening, while she was reading and her mother was watching TV, the telephone rang. It was on the table next to Mrs Anderson's chair but she left it to her daughter to answer it, frowning at the interruption during one of her favourite soaps.

Sarah reached for the handset. 'Hello?'

'Sarah?'

'Speaking.'

'It's Neal. How are you?'

'Neal...'

She had been training herself not to think about him, not to live on false hopes. His voice sounded different on the telephone. For a second or two she hadn't recognised it.

'Could you hold on a minute while I get to an extension?' Covering the mouthpiece, she said to her mother, 'Mum, give me time to get up to the office before you put this back, will you?'

Mesmerised by the screen, her mother gave an irritable nod. The characters in the soaps were as real to her as the woman who lived next door or the chiropodist who came to deal with her feet.

Sarah ran up the stairs and picked up the handset on her fax machine.

'Hello.' She was slightly breathless, more from the shock of his call than from the exertion.

Evidently he had heard the drama going on in the background. 'Have I called at a bad time?'

'No, my mother was watching the telly but I wasn't.

What a surprise to hear from you. How did you get my number?'

'I looked you up. There were only nine Andersons listed and only one with the initial S. No problem.'

'Did the rest of your trip go well?' she asked.

'Yes, it was good. How have things been with you?'

'Fine. It took a few days to settle back into the routine, but now Nepal seems quite a long time ago.'

'When can we meet?'

Night after night she had lain in bed, longing to believe that, when he came back, this was what he would say. Now she had heard him saying it but she still couldn't believe it.

'Sarah...are you still there?'

'Yes,' she said quickly. 'Just thinking. Er...I'm pretty busy at present. Christmas brings extra work.'

'How about dinner on Tuesday? I'm told by our restaurant critic that there's a very good French place a few miles north of you.'

'I believe so. I haven't been there. But I can't manage Tuesday.'

'What about Wednesday, or Thursday?'

'Hm...no, they're no good either. Besides, it's so far to come. Perhaps we could get together some time when I'm in London.'

'When is that likely to be?'

'Maybe in the New Year.'

'When were you last in London?' His tone had developed an edge.

'I don't get there very often.'

'You're stalling me, aren't you? Why?'

She should have known this wasn't going to be easy.

'Well...I think it can be a mistake for people who meet on holiday to...to try to extend the friendship. It doesn't seem to work too well.'

'That sounds like a brush-off.'

'I wouldn't put it like that.'

'I would.' He rang off.

Sarah replaced the receiver. She had achieved her objective. Why, instead of feeling relieved, did she feel like bursting into tears?

After a while, when her emotions were under control, she went downstairs. It was time for the cup of hot chocolate her mother liked at this time of the evening.

'Hot chocolate, Mum?'

'Yes, please, dear…and a biscuit.'

They had this exchange every evening. It was one of the many small rituals that made up their narrow lives. Sometimes Sarah felt that without her nocturnal wanderings on the Internet, she would go mad. The Net, and her friendship with Naomi, were her only respites from a life that she felt was stifling her. The escape to Nepal had made her restlessness worse, not better.

In his part of his parents' tall house in London, Neal was pacing the floor of a room which had once been a third-floor bedroom and was now his living room-cum-office.

It was ironic that his first brush-off had come from the first woman to give him sleepless nights.

Sarah's manner on the telephone had been so unfriendly that he couldn't believe what he was hearing. Why should she have cooled off when he hadn't?

His stint with the marathon runners had given him plenty of time to consider whether he wanted to pursue their relationship. His conclusion was that he did: that they had been so good together it would be crazy not to.

But Sarah, it seemed, had arrived at a different conclusion. Why? What was behind her aloofness and that statement about extending holiday friendships being a mistake?

That might be true in the majority of cases. But every rule had its exceptions and he felt their friendship was one of them. Because that was what it had been. A friendship.

Not only fantastic sex, but a meeting of minds on all manner of subjects and, best of all, a meeting of senses of humour. They had liked the same kind of jokes, seen the same funny side of things. But, despite that, she wanted to end it, didn't even want to have dinner with him.

For a moment or two, when she'd snubbed him with that haughty retort, 'I wouldn't put it like that,' he had lost his temper. Now he wished he hadn't rung off. It would have made more sense to press her to explain herself.

Because there had to be an explanation. Surely she couldn't imagine he was going to let it rest?

The following evening Sarah was washing up the supper things when the front door bell rang.

Mrs Anderson couldn't answer it. She had difficulty walking more than a few steps and could only reach her bedroom by means of the stair-lift Sarah had had installed.

Expecting the caller to be someone collecting for a charity, she dried her hands and went through the hall, closing the door to the lounge on her way past so that opening the front door wouldn't send a current of cold air sweeping into the warm room.

The last person she expected to find looking down at her was Neal.

'Hello again,' he said, smiling. He was carrying a large bunch of hothouse pink roses protected from the raw November night by a swathe of transparent Cellophane.

'Neal!' she said faintly, instantly aware that she looked a mess whereas he looked stunning in an expensive-looking soft dark brown leather blouson over a silver-grey cashmere turtleneck sweater.

Stepping across the threshold, he put his free arm round her, drew her close and kissed her mouth.

Immediately, all the heightened emotions she had felt in Nepal welled up inside her. The long weeks apart seemed to vanish. She was back to where she had been on their last night together: unable to contemplate a future without him.

Still holding her close, he ended the kiss and pressed his cheek against hers. 'I would have come earlier but I couldn't get away.'

'You shouldn't have come at all,' she said faintly, knowing she should push him away but unable to make herself do it.

'Why not?' Neal said, lifting his head to look down at her. 'What was all that nonsense on the phone last night?'

Before she could answer, he added, 'You'll get chilled if we go on standing here on the doormat. Let's get the door shut.'

He propelled her backwards and closed it. Then he handed over the roses and began to take off his jacket.

The way the soft cashmere moulded his powerful shoulders made Sarah's insides turn over. She had thought she was beginning to recover control of the passions he had aroused, but his presence made nonsense of that idea.

Deep down, she wanted to take his hand and lead him upstairs to her room and have him make wild love to her.

'Where can we talk?' said Neal, glancing at the closed door of the lounge through which a burst of canned laughter could be heard.

'In the kitchen,' said Sarah. 'I'll put the roses in water and make you a cup of coffee. They're beautiful. Thank you, Neal. But you shouldn't have brought them…you shouldn't be here.'

'So you keep telling me. I think it's time you gave some reasons,' he said, following her to the kitchen.

There was a stool in a recess. Sarah pulled it out for him to sit on. Then she opened a cupboard and brought out a tall cut-glass vase which was one of her mother's wedding presents.

As she took it to the sink and filled it with water, Neal

said, 'You've never talked about your home life. I'm beginning to think there is something I ought to know that you chose not to tell me.' He took in the dishes and cups in the rack on the drainer. 'Who did you eat with, Sarah? Who is it in your sitting room, listening to TV?'

'It's my mother. We live together. She's nearly seventy and a semi-invalid. She can't live on her own. I'm responsible for her. While I was away, one of our neighbours, a widow, moved in and looked after her for me. But that was a one-off, special-occasion arrangement. Mrs Evans wouldn't want to do it on a regular basis, and we couldn't afford it if she would.'

While she was talking, she filled and plugged in the kettle before turning her attention back to the roses.

'So, having no brothers and sisters, you're solely responsible for your mother's welfare,' said Neal. 'Does she object to your having relationships with other people...is that the problem?'

'No, it's not that. Mum isn't possessive. It's just that she can't be left for long. A few times Naomi, my friend and business partner, has slept here while I've been away overnight. But as a matter of principle I wouldn't impose on her kindness more than very occasionally. So you see I'm not a free agent. I can't come and go as I please.'

Neal had ignored the stool and was leaning against a worktop, his arms folded over his chest. His trousers were a darker grey than his sweater and his shoes were well-polished brown brogues with punched toecaps. He looked the personification of casual masculine elegance, making her doubly conscious that she looked a scruffy hausfrau in a sweatsuit and sneakers, without earrings, lipstick or any redeeming touches.

He came to where she was standing, putting the roses in water, and turned and tilted her face. There was nothing but kindness in his eyes. It made her want to put her arms round him and lean her head on his chest and let him take over her life. But she knew it wouldn't be right. In the long run, it would be easier for them both to cut the connection now.

'OK, so you're not as free as I am,' he said quietly. 'Is that the only reason you want to cut off our friendship?'

'The kettle is boiling.' Grateful for the reason to move away, she stepped aside to deal with it. 'Would you like coffee or tea?'

'What are you and your mother having?'

'Chocolate for Mum. Instant coffee for me.'

'Instant is fine. Have you told your mother about me?'

'No. She wouldn't approve. She finds it hard to accept modern ways and ideas.'

'A visit from someone you haven't mentioned will surprise her,' he said dryly.

'I didn't think you'd come. I didn't expect to see you again.'

'Did you really think that after our time together I wouldn't get in touch?'

'I wasn't sure.' She gave him a direct look. 'Were you? When we said goodbye at the airport, did you intend then to see me again?'

'I wasn't sure either,' he conceded. 'Away from one's normal surroundings, it's easy to get carried away. I knew that I'd never forget you. It was more than a casual affair. But I didn't know then how much more. I do now. I want to see a lot more of you, Sarah. I want us to spend time together...to get to know each other properly. At the moment we could be described as intimate strangers.'

Hope fluttered to life inside her. *Was* there a future for them? An instant later she knew it could never work. He only knew half the problem. There was more to it...so much more.

At that moment she heard her mother's voice. 'Sarah...?'

Although, since the failure of the second operation on

her knee, Mrs Anderson had been unable to walk unaided, she could hobble about the lounge with the aid of her stick and holding onto the furniture.

Now, when Sarah answered her call, her mother was holding onto the upright piano which had always stood in the lounge although it had never been played by anyone but her long-dead grandmother.

'I thought I heard a man's voice, dear? It's not Matthew, is it?'

Sarah shook her head. 'It's a friend…someone I met in Nepal.' She looked over her shoulder. 'Neal, come and meet my mother.'

He came to join them, offering his hand and smiling.

'Hello, Mrs Anderson.'

'Oh…pleased to meet you.' Visibly taken aback by the unexpected appearance of this intensely virile stranger, Dolly Anderson put her little plump, pallid hand into his large, hard, brown one.

He shook hands gently, Sarah noticed. There could hardly be a more marked contrast between any two people than between these two: the tall, active, confident man and the small, semi-invalid, timorous woman.

'You must forgive me for bursting in on you like this,' Neal said to her. 'I'm bringing an invitation from my mother. She would like Sarah to spend a weekend with us. Perhaps you would like to come too. Shall we all sit down and discuss it?'

Transferring her hand to his left one and putting his other arm round her, he steered her back to the chair where she had been sitting.

Dumbfounded, Sarah followed. Did the invitation really come from his mother, or had he made it up on the spur of the moment? She was torn between gratification that he wanted her to meet his family and despair at what must ensue. Even if, at the moment, he couldn't see, or chose to disregard, the obstacles between them, his family would certainly recognise them.

'Well, I don't know, Mr...er...' her mother said, still confused, as she sank into her chair.

'My surname's Kennedy, but please call me Neal.'

He sat down at the end of the sofa nearest to her, leaning forward, all his attention focused on a woman who must, Sarah thought, be as different from his own mother as a portly tabby from a sleek Siamese.

'You see, Neal, I never go out...except in the garden, in summer. Getting about is too much for me.'

'I'm sorry to hear that. What's the problem?'

Oh, God, here we go, Sarah thought, helpless to stem the outpouring of medical details he had invited. She left them to it and went to the kitchen to finish making the coffee and her mother's hot drink.

By the time she returned with the tray, which Neal sprang up to take from her, Mrs Anderson was in full flow, relating what Matthew called 'all the gory details', meaning an exhaustive description of her operation and its aftermath.

When eating a biscuit silenced her, Neal said, 'Providing you don't have to over-exert yourself, a weekend away could do you a power of good. I'm the medical correspondent for *The Journal* newspaper. If I have a word with your doctor, I'm sure I can get him to agree to letting you come. Who is he?'

Mrs Anderson told him. 'Are you a doctor yourself?' she asked.

'Not a practising one...or not unless there's an emergency. Excuse me a moment. I just want to get my palmtop and jot those details down.'

As he left the room, Mrs Anderson said in a stage whisper, 'What a nice man. You never mentioned meeting him out there.'

'I met lots of people, Mum.'

'Not many like him, I'm sure,' said Mrs Anderson roguishly. 'He must have taken to you to come all this way.'

To Sarah's embarrassment, Neal overheard this remark. 'Your daughter's a charmer, Mrs Anderson...and now I can see whose genes made her that way,' he added.

It was such an outrageous bit of flirting that, if Sarah hadn't been burning with annoyance, she would have been forced to laugh.

Her mother's reaction was to giggle. As she watched him key in her doctor's name on a pocket-size organiser, she said, 'Sarah's keen on all these modern gadgets. So is—'

Desperate to stop her saying what she sensed was coming next, Sarah cut in, 'Don't you think you should check with *your* mother, Neal, before you bring two guests home?'

He gave her a look of amused understanding. 'I live under my parents' roof but not *with* them, Sarah. I left home a long time ago but moved back the year before last because they needed help with their overheads. The house is too big for them now, but they don't want to move. So I converted the top floors into flats for myself and my grandfather. He was getting too old to live on his own so the arrangement suited everyone.'

He turned to her mother. 'I notice you have a stair-lift, Mrs Anderson. We put in a lift for Grandpa. I'll move down to his guest room while you're with us, and you and Sarah can sleep in my flat. How does that sound?'

'It sounds very exciting. You won't believe it but I've never been to London.'

'Really? Then it's high time you came,' he said warmly. 'What time do you usually go to bed, Mrs Anderson?'

'I'm a night owl,' she told him. 'Sarah gets up very early, but I like to stay up late and watch television. Not all that nasty stuff they put on after nine o'clock. I mostly watch videos.'

'In that case I'm sure you won't mind if I take Sarah out for an hour. I've checked in at a hotel on the other side of town. It has a pleasant bar where we can have a drink. Then I'll bring her back.'

'I'm not dressed for going out,' Sarah said tensely.

'Then run and get yourself ready, dear,' said her mother. 'I'll keep Neal company.'

Although she objected strongly to being manipulated, Sarah wasn't averse to the chance to tell Neal, in private, precisely what she thought of these unfair manoeuvres.

What was worrying her, as she shot upstairs to her bedroom, was what her mother might tell him in her absence. Mrs Anderson had been on the point of mentioning Matthew when Sarah had interrupted her.

She particularly didn't want Neal to hear about her son from anyone but her. But it would be just like her mother, who doted on Matthew, to start extolling him to Neal, unaware that he knew nothing about him.

CHAPTER EIGHT

BY THE time she came downstairs, after transforming herself with a speed a quick-change artist would have been pressed to beat, Sarah was fizzing like the champagne that, for some reason she could never fathom, victorious sportsmen shook up and sprayed over everyone near them.

However, when she entered the lounge, there was nothing in Neal's expression to suggest that he had just been told something surprising, even shocking about her.

'I won't keep her out late, Mrs Anderson,' he said, rising.

'Sarah's a grown woman, dear. She comes and goes as she pleases,' said her mother.

He took her hand between his. 'Then I'll say goodnight. It's been a pleasure meeting you.'

'Hypocrite!' Sarah glowered at him, as they paused in the hall for him to put on his jacket.

He had closed the lounge door behind him, so there was no danger of her mother overhearing her comment.

'What makes you say that?' he asked.

She reserved her reply until they were going down the path. 'Because the chasm between you and my mother is as wide as the Grand Canyon. You have absolutely nothing in common.'

'On the contrary, we have a mutual interest in you,' he said easily. 'That's not a bad start. Do you come and go as you please? I wouldn't think so.'

'I don't know what you mean by that?'

His car was parked with the passenger door by the kerb. It had central locking. He opened the door for her.

It wasn't until he was in the driver's seat that he said,

'I mean that I think you have allowed your mother's disability to dominate both your lives. After spending a short time with her, I can see she's a couch potato and that isn't good for anyone. You, I suspect, suffer from one of the syndromes that carers are prone to. You're resigning yourself to a life that is too circumscribed. From what she's told me, the trip to Nepal was the first time in years that you've had a proper holiday...and you had to be bullied into taking it by your friend Naomi.'

'I can't believe what I'm hearing,' Sarah exploded. 'You barge back into my life, when I've made it clear I don't want you, and you have the crass gall to tell me that I'm not running it right. I...I...' She struggled for words to express the force of her anger.

Neal's response was so quiet as to be almost a murmur. 'You don't want me, Sarah?'

He didn't wait for her reply. The next instant she was in his arms, being kissed with a passion as explosive as her anger.

At first she struggled, beating her clenched fists against his leather-clad shoulders and trying to wrench her mouth away. But he had his fingers in her hair, holding her head still. She couldn't escape the devouring heat of his mouth. It wasn't long before she no longer wanted to. Her body, flooding with desire, began to relax in his arms, her lips to soften, to yield and, finally, to respond.

He was the one to end it. Looking down at her, his eyes glittering, he said in a husky rasp, 'You want me, Sarah. You want me as much as I want you.'

Then he let her go and started the car.

They were halfway to the hotel, the only good one the town had, before she felt even halfway back in control of her feelings. They were on the ring road by now, but not travelling fast. In the sudden flare of light from the headlamps of a vehicle overtaking them, she saw that his jaw was clenched. But his hands weren't gripping the wheel. They were relaxed and sure.

It amazed her that he could drive. She knew she wasn't fit to. Her concentration was so shot that she doubted if she could perform the most automatic routines.

The neon-lit sign marking the turn-in to the hotel was now in sight. Sarah had been there only once before, almost a year ago, when Naomi had organised a Christmas drinks party for their best customers.

There were parking spaces for short-stay drivers in front of the hotel, and a larger parking area for patrons behind the building. Neal drove round to the back.

They entered the reception lounge through the draught lobby at the rear. As he held the inner door for her to pass through, she was met by the ambience peculiar to good hotels designed to attract upper-echelon business travellers. In addition to excessive central heating, the atmosphere was a blend of cigars, costly shaving lotions and wet oasis from the elaborate arrangements of otherwise scentless flowers.

Remembering where the bar was, because she and Naomi had had a bracer there before the party, she was moving in that direction when Neal caught her by the hand and led her into an open lift.

'We'll talk in my room. It will be quieter.'

Sarah wasn't happy about this, but his hold on her hand was too firm to shake off and just then they were joined by another person whose presence restrained her objection.

As the lift doors slid shut and they were carried upwards, she realised that a public bar wasn't the ideal place to have a heated exchange on a very personal subject. The privacy of his room *would* be better, provided...

Her reservations were still unspecified when the doors slid back, revealing the first-floor corridor. The other passenger stepped out and they followed him, but turned in the opposite direction.

Even when they reached his door, Neal didn't release her hand. He had taken a slip of plastic from an inside pocket of his jacket. It released the lock on his door. He pushed it open, switched on a light and waited for her to precede him.

By Sarah's standards, the room was luxuriously comfortable with a king-size double divan and two armchairs on either side of a low table. One side of the bed had been turned down, and a chocolate and a fresh flower laid on the pillow.

'Let me take your coat,' said Neal.

Somewhat reluctantly, she unbuttoned the hip-length wool coat she had flung on over a jersey dress. Neal helped her take it off and laid it over the back of an upright chair at a writing table equipped with a leather blotter and a rack of hotel stationery.

Turning back to her, his eyes warm, his mouth starting to smile, he said, 'Sorry about that rather rough kiss in the car. I lost my temper...something I don't often do.'

'I lost mine too,' she conceded. 'But that doesn't alter the fact that you shouldn't have come here. There's no future for us, Neal. You know that as well as I do.'

He came closer, putting his hands on her shoulders. 'I don't know any such thing. I know that we want each other. We've had time to cool off, but we haven't. The minute I saw you again, I wanted to take you to bed, and that's what I'm going to do...right now.'

'No...no...' Her attempt to back off and her protest were both futile. His arms enfolded her, his mouth closed over hers, and she was lost. The arousal she'd felt in the car needed only the smallest contact to set it off again. Her mind resisted, but her body betrayed her.

For weeks she had been longing for him, starving for him, and now she was in his arms, alone in a room where no one would disturb them, with soft lights and a comfortable bed. It was madness. It was wrong. It could only make matters worse. But she couldn't do a thing to stop it.

Afterwards, when Neal had gone to the bathroom, she sat up and looked at their scattered clothes and then at the signs of their wild love-making on her body. I must be mad, she thought. How could I have done that?

They were almost the same thoughts she had had long ago, she remembered. The circumstances were different, but the feelings were almost identical, except that all those long years ago they had been shot through with panic in case there were consequences too frightening even to think about.

This time that wouldn't happen. She could almost wish that it would. Although her intelligence told her it would be an act of insanity, in her soul she longed for Neal's child. But even if there were no other obstacles, it would be unwise. The older the mother, the higher the risks, or so it was said by the experts. But sometimes the experts were wrong.

Neal came back, wearing a white terry bath robe. He unzipped an overnight case lying on the luggage stand and produced something dark and silky. He tossed it onto the bed.

'Do you want to put that on? I'm going to call Room Service. What would you like to drink? Wine?'

When she nodded, he punched in some numbers on the telephone keypad and had a quick look at a menu standing on the night table.

Sarah reached for what turned out to be his robe. It drowned her but it gave her a deep secret pleasure to wear it, even for a short time. She listened to Neal ordering cold beef and smoked salmon sandwiches, a litre bottle of mineral water and a sophisticated-sounding wine.

'Hadn't I better be dressed when the room waiter comes?' she asked. 'Are guests allowed to have women in their rooms?'

'I wouldn't know,' said Neal. 'This isn't a situation I've ever been in before. If I had my way, you'd call your mother and tell her you're staying the night, and I'd change my reservation from one person in a double room to two people in a double.'

'You know that's impossible.'

'Is it?' He leaned across the bed, captured her hand and held the palm to his cheek. 'Is it really impossible?'

She reclaimed her hand. 'You know it is. I can't leave Mum alone. She has no idea that we...that we're on these terms. It would come as a horrible shock to her. She has old-fashioned ideas.'

'If she spends her life watching TV, she can't be that old-fashioned. The soaps aren't behind the times,' he said dryly.

'Seeing things in soaps isn't the same as suddenly finding out that her daughter is spending nights with a man she didn't know existed until this evening. I must get dressed.'

'Must you? I like you *en déshabillé*...it's nice being able to reach out and touch my favourite parts of you.' He demonstrated by slipping his hand between the lapels of the robe and stroking one of her breasts.

Sarah recoiled as if a stranger had caressed her. Yet not very long ago she had welcomed his hands and lips on her.

'You're not being fair,' she protested. 'You brought me here, knowing I didn't want this to happen. Oh, all right—' as he raised a sardonic eyebrow '—part of me wanted it. But not the sensible part.'

Snatching up her clothes, she made for the bathroom.

While she was there, she heard the floor waiter bringing the things Neal had ordered. She waited until she heard him say, 'Thank you, sir. Goodnight, sir,' before she opened the door.

There was now a tray on the table, with a bottle of wine in an ice bucket, a vacuum jug presumably containing the spring water, one wine glass and one gold-rimmed plate with a knife and a linen napkin beside it, and a silver dish containing two rows of brown sandwiches garnished with parsley, curls of lemon and black olives.

Neal, who had risen from a chair, gestured for her to take the other. He filled the glass of wine and handed it to her.

'But that's your glass.'

'I'll use a glass from the bathroom.' He went to fetch one.

Her eyes slid over his back view from the broad brown shoulders to the lean hips and sexy backside under the tightly wrapped towel. She knew she was looking at him in the lustful way men looked at girls.

Was it only lust that she felt? The lubricious need of a woman long starved of physical release? Was she deluding herself that her feelings towards him were on a higher, finer plane?

Neal came back and poured wine for himself. He offered her the dish of sandwiches.

'I've already had supper.'

'Have one to keep me company.'

She took one and drank some wine. 'Neal…this invitation you talked about…I think you made it up.'

'Why would I do that?'

'I'm not sure…a kind impulse maybe.'

'I'm not impulsive or kind. I want you to come for a weekend and the only way you're going to do that is if your mother comes too. It would be good for her. I'll drive up early one morning and on the way back we can stop for lunch somewhere.'

'We couldn't possibly put you to all that trouble. If we

came, we'd do it by train. Naomi would run us to the station.'

'It's agreed, then?'

'I don't know. I need to think about it.' She drank some more wine. 'We're avoiding the issue. It didn't matter in Nepal. We were strangers who happened to meet and had a good time together. But now we're on home ground it's different. You know what I mean. I shouldn't have to spell it out.'

He put down his untouched glass and leaned towards her. 'You'll have to. I may be dense, but I haven't a clue what you're getting at.' He appeared to be genuinely mystified.

She drew a breath. 'I'm older than you are.'

'Oh...that.' He gave a slight shrug, as if he had been expecting some quite different revelation. 'Why is that an issue? You're a few years older...so what?'

'It's more than a few years, Neal. It's eleven years.'

'You're forty-seven? I wouldn't have guessed it. I thought forty...maybe forty-one. You have some good genes going for you. They sometimes skip generations.'

Sarah leaned back in her chair and gave an audible sigh. 'You dismiss it as if it's not important.'

'Is it?' he asked.

'You know it is, Neal.'

He picked up his wine. 'If I were your age and you were mine, would it be important?'

'That's a different matter. Our culture accepts older men and younger women...not the other way round.'

'That argument doesn't hold water. Our culture is riddled with cant and dubious values. People who think for themselves work out their own code of behaviour. I think what you mean is that *you* aren't comfortable with the age difference. I am.'

'You may not be the first time you hear someone murmur something about toy boys.'

He threw back his head and laughed. The lines of his long strong neck and the glimpse of his white teeth sent a flash of pleasure through her.

'Toy boys are like bimbos, Sarah. They have distinguishing marks. I'm never going to be mistaken for one of them. Nor do you look anything like the kind of woman who has a toy boy in tow.'

Sarah was on the point of retorting that the age gap might not hit people in the eye now but would become more noticeable as time went on, when it struck her that he might not be contemplating anything but a short-term relationship.

The distinction between lust and love had been in her mind minutes earlier. Perhaps, as far as he was concerned, love wasn't on the agenda. Yet, if that were so, why did he want her to meet his family and vice versa?

Neal drank some wine and bit into one of the sandwiches. Before taking another bite, he said, 'You take life altogether too seriously. That often happens to people whose lives are constricted by circumstances outside their control...in your case by having to care for an elderly mother. You were out of your shell in Nepal. Don't go back inside it now.'

She thought how lovely it would be if she *could* spend the night here, and wake in his arms, and have breakfast with him, the way they had in Nepal. But that was impossible now.

'I must go,' she said.

'OK. Have some more wine while I'm getting dressed.'

He would have topped up her glass but Sarah put her fingers over the top. 'There's no need...I'll get a taxi.'

'You will not,' he said firmly. 'I brought you. I'll take you home.' He took her chin in his hand and swooped down to kiss her.

Sarah watched him dress, putting his arms into the sleeves of his sweater and then pulling it over his head in the same way that Matthew did. She still hadn't told him about Matthew but somehow that seemed a huge hurdle which she couldn't tackle tonight.

'When are you leaving?' she asked.

'After we've had brunch tomorrow. I'll pick you up about nine. I'm sure your mother will understand that I'd like to have you to myself for a few hours.'

Neal didn't come to the door with her. He kissed her good-night in the car, then stayed watching her walk up the path and only switched on his engine after she had unlocked the door and turned on the hall light.

The TV was on in the lounge, but the screen was blank when Sarah put her head round the door. For the first time in Sarah's memory her mother had zapped a film.

'I didn't expect you back yet, dear. Did you have a nice time?'

Sarah wondered how her mother would react if she told her the truth: that she and Neal had been to bed together. With shock and distaste probably. Her parents' marriage had been a master and slave relationship. Her father had never shown kindness or tenderness downstairs. It wasn't likely he had been a different man upstairs.

She said, 'We had wine and sandwiches. Neal wants me to spend some time with him tomorrow, Mum. From about nine till three. Is that all right with you?'

'Of course it is, dear. I liked him *very* much. Why didn't you tell me you'd met someone special?'

'It's just a friendship, Mum. It's no big deal. Did you mention Matthew when you were talking to Neal while I was changing?'

'I don't think so. I can't remember. Haven't you told him about Matthew?'

'Not yet. Weren't you watching a film until you heard the front door?'

'Yes, but it was a load of rubbish. I'd rather talk to you.'

'I'm tired. Can I get you anything before I go up?'

'No, I think I'll come up too. I've got a nice library book I want to finish. You do look a bit worn out. You don't want shadows under your eyes tomorrow.'

Back in his room at the hotel, Neal switched on the TV and tuned in to CNN News. He poured himself some more wine and began to undress for the second time that evening, this time hanging his clothes up. Then he relaxed on the bed, the pillows stacked behind him.

But although he was watching the screen and part of his mind was taking in the world news seen from the US angle, he was also thinking about Sarah and her difficult situation as the sole support of her mother.

It had been no more or less than the truth when he told her the difference in their ages was a matter of indifference to him. But whether his family might share Sarah's concern was hard to say. After the anguish they had suffered over Chris's marriage and his subsequent death, Neal didn't want to cause them any further anxiety.

Then there was the aspect of her past that Sarah was still holding back. Every time they made love, he was reminded that she wasn't being totally open and honest with him. That worried him. It seemed to mean that she didn't trust him.

Perhaps she would tell him tomorrow. If she didn't, he would have to tell her that he knew she had had a child. They couldn't go on any longer with her past a no-go area.

Lying in the bath, the next morning, Sarah resolved that today she would put all her cards on the table. If, in doing so, she put Neal off her, that was a risk she must take.

If he saw their relationship as a pleasant affair that might last for some time but not for ever, then what had happened in the past wouldn't matter to him. But if he was beginning to be serious, and there were times when she thought he might be, then his reaction was less predictable.

And Matthew's reaction to Neal was even more of a wild card. Thank goodness he wasn't at home at the moment. But it wouldn't be long before he was back. And she was fairly certain he wouldn't share her mother's attitude to Neal. Even Mum's attitude could change. She had always been easily influenced. If Matthew took against Neal he could easily convert his doting granny to his point of view.

Sarah dressed and made up with care. With a plastic apron over her best outfit, a classic round-necked suit of fudge-coloured gabardine, she prepared her mother's lunch. The parts that needed heating would only take a few minutes in the microwave.

Mrs Anderson had spent years cooking traditional meals for a husband who wouldn't touch 'foreign muck' or salads. After his death, she had given up cooking, leaving it all to Sarah who tried to provide them both with a balanced diet. But her mother's sedentary life and weakness for fancy biscuits conspired against her losing weight.

Sarah was watching from the lounge window when she saw Neal's car pull up outside their garden gate.

'He's here, Mum. I'll see you later. Cheerio.' She gave her mother a quick kiss and hurried to the front door.

Neal was at the gate as she closed it behind her.

'I thought, as it's fine, we might drive into the country and go for a walk,' he said. 'Are those shoes all right for walking?'

She had dressed for lunching at his hotel which was a weekend rendezvous for the town's well-to-do people. She never wore very high heels, but the shoes she had on weren't ideal for a country ramble.

'I'll bring some flat heels. I won't be two minutes,' she

said, wanting to stop him having another tête-à-tête with
her mother until later on, when he knew all the circumstances of their family life.

'Bring a coat as well. You might need it over your suit,'
he suggested, remaining by the gate.

When they were both in the car, he leaned over and
kissed her. 'Good morning. You're looking very smart.'

'Only by contrast with the travelling gear you've seen
me in so far. I thought it was time I brought out my other
persona…the efficient businesswoman,' she said, smiling.
'Where are we going? You didn't tell me you knew this
part of the world?'

'I don't, but the hall porter does. I told him I wanted
to stroll with someone who might not be keen on footpaths
through fields of cows. He's given me directions for a
river walk. I missed you last night.' He took one hand off
the wheel, reached for one of hers and gave it a squeeze.

'I would have liked to stay,' Sarah admitted. 'Neal, I
have things to tell you…things I should have told you
before.'

'Wait till we get there. Then I can give you my full
attention,' he said.

She was fairly sure where they were going. It was one
of the region's beauty spots: a stretch of quiet-flowing
river with low hills in the background. If that *was* their
destination, it would be a strange twist of fate that brought
her back to a place where once she had walked with someone else important to her.

Neal parked the car on the outskirts of a village. 'According to my directions, if we cut down that lane we'll
find ourselves by the river,' he said.

Sarah changed her shoes and put on the shower coat
she had brought. 'Could I put my bag in the boot?' she
asked.

'Good idea.' He unlocked it for her.

When they reached the footpath, the pale wintry sun-

light was making the river gleam and a moorhen was pad-
dling about among the sedges by the far bank.

'Nice spot,' said Neal. 'Which way shall we go? Left
or right?'

'Right,' said Sarah.

'You've been here before, I expect?'

'Yes, but a long time ago. I was still in my teens the
last time I came here.'

He took her hand in his. 'What is it you want to tell
me?'

She swallowed, her throat dry with nervousness. 'I've
never been married...but I have a son.'

Neal's fingers tightened on hers as if he guessed it was
difficult for her to talk about it. 'What happened to his
father?'

'He was killed on his motorbike. His name was Matt.
He was the boy next door. I'd known him all my life, but
my father didn't approve of him. Dad didn't approve of
most people. He was a difficult man who ruled us like a
Roman paterfamilias. What he thought and said was law.'

'What was Matt's particular crime?' Neal asked.

'Being young and perhaps a bit wild...but no more than
most boys of that age. Like me, he was an only child and
his parents adored him. His father paid the down payment
on his bike and his mother bought him black leathers. But
he wasn't the spoilt brat that Dad made him out to be. He
was remarkably unspoilt. Everyone liked Matt.'

'And you loved him,' Neal said quietly.

'Yes, I thought he was wonderful. When Dad stopped
him coming round to see us, it made me very unhappy.'

'Did your mother disapprove of Matt?'

'She liked him, but she never disagreed with Dad. She
was afraid of him,' Sarah said bleakly.

'Were you?'

After a pause, she said, 'Yes. I was glad when he
died...glad Matthew didn't have to grow up in that atmo-

sphere. I've come to terms with it now…the fact that I hated my father. But when I was young I felt terribly guilty about it.'

'I can imagine,' said Neal. 'How did you and Matt manage to get together if your father wouldn't have him in the house?'

'We met when he was on duty or away from home. He was away quite a lot, at conferences and things. Sometimes I slipped out at night, after Mum was in bed. I didn't like doing things by stealth, but I couldn't see why I shouldn't have the fun other girls were enjoying. Then one night, when I wasn't with him, Matt had an accident.'

She could speak of it calmly now, although it would always hurt her to think of Matt's life snuffed out when he'd hardly begun to live.

'He was in Intensive Care for three days. Then he died. Perhaps it was better that way. He had terrible injuries to his legs. I wasn't allowed to see him. The whole street— apart from my father—was upset by his death. So it was all right to have red eyes. Mum had them too…all the women we knew were crying for him.'

'Oh, Sarah!' There was a world of compassion in Neal's exclamation. He drew her close and hugged her. 'How old were you when this happened?'

She leaned against him, grateful for his understanding. 'I was seventeen…nearly eighteen. Two weeks after Matt's funeral, I missed my period. We had only made love a few times and Matt said it would be all right but somehow it wasn't. For six weeks I lived in terror of what Dad would say when I told him. I considered running away. But I had nowhere to go and I knew what could happen to girls who left home without any money. So I sat it out until my shape started changing. Then I had to tell him.'

She straightened, withdrawing from his arms, her face

calm. 'By then I was fairly sure that he wouldn't throw me out because it would make him look bad in the eyes of his colleagues. I was right about that...but, oh, God, the explosion of anger! After that, he ignored me. For the rest of his life, he never spoke to me. Even when I came out of hospital with Matthew, it was as if we didn't exist. Not many people can resist a new baby, but Dad did.'

'It sounds to me as if your father was mentally disturbed,' said Neal. 'Whatever was wrong with him was probably curable, but the diagnosis and treatment of mental illnesses wasn't as good then as now.'

'There's one more bad thing I must tell you,' Sarah said heavily. 'Some years after his death, there was an enquiry into the alleged mistreatment of people held at the police station where he worked. He was implicated. I've sometimes thought that perhaps he vented his angry feelings towards me by being brutal to people brought in for questioning.'

Neal put both hands on her shoulders. 'It's all long over and done with. I'm glad you've told me. I knew you were holding back something. I knew that you'd had a child.'

'You knew? How could you know?'

'There's a very faint line of pigmentation running down from your navel to your mons veneris. It would have appeared in the early stages of your pregnancy. In some women it fades completely after they've given birth. In others it's always detectable. I noticed it the first time we made love.'

Sarah digested this. 'You must have thought me very devious,' she said, in a low voice.

'No...I guessed that you'd been through some trauma you would only confide to someone you trusted without reservation. I'm glad we've reached that point.' He bent his head and brushed a kiss on her forehead.

'It's not a very pretty story. I didn't want to put you off me,' she admitted.

'Why would it do that? You were a victim of circumstance. It wasn't your fault that you were debarred from enjoying all the normal teenage pleasures. If Matt hadn't been killed, you would most likely have married and lived happily ever afterwards. You would be here with him, not me.'

'Yes, possibly. Except that I'm not sure I loved him in the way that lasts a lifetime. It was probably only calf love.'

'Is Matthew like his father?'

'Yes, in looks he's the image of him. But not in temperament. Matt hated school and left as soon as he could. Matthew is clever. He went to university.'

'Where is he now?' Neal asked.

'The last time he sent us a postcard, he was in a place called Coyhaique in Patagonia. He said he would be home for Christmas. He left home last New Year's Day to spend a year seeing the world. It's been a long year for us...for Mum and me.'

'He'll have had some marvellous adventures. He'll talk your ear off for days,' Neal remarked, smiling.

'I expect so.' She paused. 'But I don't think he'll be too pleased to find that I'm in a relationship with someone who's only seven years older than he is. He's twenty-nine, Neal. He's closer to your age than I am.'

CHAPTER NINE

'HAS he reacted badly to your other relationships?' Neal asked.

'There haven't been many. They were both a long time ago and very short-lived. He wasn't aware they happened.'

'Are you saying that he thinks his father was and remains the only man in your life?'

'I think so.'

'In that case, if he loves you, he must be concerned about you. It's unnatural for any woman not to have a man in her life. For one as lovely as you are, it's crazy.'

'I don't think children, even grown-up children, are ever very comfortable with the idea of their parents' sexuality,' said Sarah. 'Especially not sons with their mothers. They see them as mothers...not as women.'

'Maybe, but sooner or later they have to adjust that perception. I'm sure Matthew is mature enough to want whatever is best for you.'

'I hope so,' she said uncertainly.

'What does he do for a living?'

'He hasn't quite got to that stage yet. He has a good degree...good enough to get him a place on a couple of grant-aided postgraduate study courses. He went on building up his qualifications until he was twenty-five and then he looked for a job. But he couldn't get what he wanted. There were too many equally well-qualified people chasing too few vacancies. He's had various temporary jobs, but none of them with the prospects he feels entitled to. Hence his present "sabbatical". We're hoping the situation has improved since his last stint of job-hunting.'

'What's the field he's interested in?' Neal asked.

'He wants to go into politics...not as a Member of Parliament but behind the scenes. It's a difficult field to break into...'

She stopped short of adding 'unless you have contacts at Westminster who can pull strings for you' in case Neal should think she was hoping he might know powerful people.

'Why is he attracted to politics? Is he an idealist? Does he want to change the world for the better?'

'Doesn't everyone?' Sarah asked.

She couldn't be sure, but she thought there had been a faint edge of sarcasm in Neal's questions. Any criticism of Matthew, even implied, made her spring to his defence. Perhaps it was a universal maternal reflex. She knew her son wasn't perfect. But when other people were critical of him, instinctively she defended him.

When Neal made no comment on her answer, she went on, 'Matthew's hero at school was the head boy. It was Guy who inspired him to try for a place at university. Guy is now in his middle thirties. Last year he was appointed principal private secretary to the Prime Minister. If anyone wields power and influence, he does.'

'I've read about him,' said Neal. 'It's always been the faceless men in government departments who exert the real power. Political parties come and go, but the civil servants hang in there and continue their manipulations with a new set of puppets.'

'You're very cynical.'

'I've met quite a lot of power-mongers...the politicians and their so-called servants. With some exceptions, they're not the cream of the human race. Maybe, when Matthew comes home, you'll find his aspirations have changed. Seeing the world often has that effect.'

'Maybe.' Already she had a sinking feeling that Matthew and Neal were not going to take to each other.

'How did he raise the money for his trip?'

'When he couldn't get a foot on his career ladder, he decided to look for work which paid well because not many people would do it. It's surprising how many of those kind of jobs there are.'

'That shows grit,' said Neal.

Sarah chose not to mention that an added inducement had been her promise to match Matthew's earnings, pound for pound, from her own. It had been a struggle but she had felt it was worth it. She had wanted her son to have the travel opportunities she had missed—until the prize trip to Nepal had fallen out of the sky.

'What about his father's family?' Neal asked. 'Have they been supportive?'

'Soon after Matt was killed, they moved away…right away. His mother couldn't stand the reminders. Later on, after Dad died, I found out where they had gone and went to see them. I thought it might help them to know about Matthew. To my amazement, they'd split up and were living with new partners. I only saw Matthew's mother and it was obvious I wasn't welcome. I couldn't believe it.'

Neal put an arm round her shoulders. 'You've really had a rough time. It's amazing you've come through so well. As for Matt's parents' split, it's not as unusual as you might think. Tragedies like that either draw people closer together or show up concealed flaws in a relationship. Often what happens is that one of them blames the other for whatever happened. It may be that his mother blamed his father for helping him to buy the motorbike.'

'Yes, I think she did…but I still don't understand why she wasn't interested in her grandson.'

'Strange, I agree,' said Neal. 'Perhaps the only way she could deal with her son's death was by closing her mind to it. Matt's child would have been a reminder of something unbearable. You're a strong woman, Sarah. You've proved that. Not everyone has your guts.'

He turned her into his arms and kissed her with great tenderness.

'It's turning colder and there are clouds building up. Let's go back to the hotel.'

At the hotel, they had coffee in the main lounge. The building was new but the lounge had been decorated in the style of a country house library with the walls either panelled with wood or lined with rows of old leather-bound books.

Sarah was thinking what a restful atmosphere this created when Naomi walked in, accompanied by a man in his fifties. Sarah recognised him as a prominent local businessman.

Naomi spotted her. After a moment of visible surprise, she said something to her companion and brought him over.

'Hello...I didn't expect to find you here. Royce, this is my partner, Sarah Anderson.'

He offered his hand. 'My pleasure, Ms Anderson.'

Wondering what he was doing with Naomi, she shook hands and smiled. Turning to Neal, she said, 'Mr Baring is the chairman of our major industry and a prominent member of the town council.' Turning to him, she added, 'Mr Kennedy comes from London. He's a well-known journalist.'

Wringing the younger man's hand, Royce Baring said, 'I thought I recognised your face. You write for *The Journal*—yes? My mother has more faith in you than in her own doctor. She sends me clippings from your column when you deal with what she considers my health problems.'

Neal laughed. 'You look very fit to me.'

'I try to keep in shape, yes.' He turned to Sarah. 'I met your partner at a very dull civic reception. I was chatting her up when she started trying to convince me that what my business needs is a website. We arranged to have lunch and discuss the matter more fully.' The twinkle in his eyes made it clear that it wasn't Naomi's professional expertise he was chiefly interested in.

Sarah remembered hearing that he was divorced and had a succession of good-looking girlfriends.

She said pleasantly, 'Every business needs a presence on the Internet, Mr Baring. It's where the action is.'

He chuckled. To Neal, he said, 'What brings you to these backwoods, Kennedy? Business or pleasure?'

Neal said, 'Pleasure,' and smiled at Sarah.

'In that case, we won't intrude. Nice meeting you.' Baring took Naomi's arm and steered her to an empty sofa in a distant corner of the large room.

They had both risen to greet the others. As they sat down, Neal said, 'I like your friend, but I'm not so sure about him. Looks a bit of a wolf to me.'

'You could be right, but Naomi can cope with wolves. She's also a brilliant saleswoman. Before we went into business together, she'd done all kinds of selling from seasonal demos in big stores to slogging round the county persuading farmers to buy fire extinguishers.'

'How did you meet?'

'At an exercise class for pregnant mums. Naomi was married, but it didn't last long. She brought up her daughter pretty well single-handed. You wouldn't think it to look at her but she's a grandmother. Her daughter Alice had a baby last year.'

As she spoke, Sarah half-regretted adding that information. It underlined the fact that she could also be a grandmother. Which might not be off-putting to someone of Royce Baring's age, but must give Neal cause to think.

But it seemed Neal had something else on his mind. He said, 'It's not half past twelve yet. I booked a table for one-thirty. Let's go up to my room.'

As they left the lounge, Sarah wondered if Naomi had

noticed their departure and, when they reappeared in the restaurant in an hour's time, would draw the inevitable conclusion that they had been to bed. Not that it would come as a surprise since Sarah had already made it clear the affair had started in Nepal. She regretted that now. For reasons she couldn't analyse, she would have preferred to keep their relationship private.

Going up in the lift, Neal said, 'I spoke to my mother this morning. She and Dad have a date next weekend, but the following weekend is clear, if that's OK for you?'

'All our weekends are clear,' she said wryly.

'It shouldn't be like that. You should be meeting people…getting about…having fun.' He stroked her cheek with the backs of his fingers. 'I want to give you a good time…make up for all that you've missed.'

Seconds after closing the door of his room, he took her in his arms and began the sweet, slow build-up to a crescendo of passion that left Sarah exhausted and contented.

'Let's not go down,' he murmured, close to her ear. 'Let's have something sent up. It's going to seem a long two weeks before I see you again.'

'We shan't be able to do this in your parents' house,' she said drowsily.

He stroked some stray locks of hair from her damp forehead. 'You won't be staying in their house. You'll be in my flat. I have it all worked out. I shall doctor your mother's nightcap and, when she's out for the count, I'll come and have my way with you.'

In a different way, his teasing made her as happy as his love-making. She had missed out on all foolish, tender jokes which were an essential part of a close relationship.

Neal drove back to London with an easier mind. It was clear to him now why Sarah had tried to brush him off on the telephone. He could even understand her motive. But what she saw as insuperable obstacles, he saw as minor difficulties.

He couldn't deny that it would have been a lot simpler if she had been free, as he was, to come and go as she pleased. But she wasn't, and he could cope with that.

If anyone was going to be a problem, it was more likely to be the son than the elderly mother. From what Sarah had told him about Matthew, Neal took him to be a bit of a loafer, one of those bright but inherently lazy characters who, if the grants were forthcoming, would happily go on taking postgraduate courses and avoiding the moment when they had to buckle down to the grind of earning an unsubsidised living.

Times were tough, but not *that* tough, he thought, shifting into fifth gear to cruise down the south-bound motorway. If Matthew was as bright as Sarah claimed, he could have found himself a job before now. Taking off for a year was fine at nineteen, but twenty-nine was too old for that sort of lark. The guy should be taking the weight off his mother's shoulders, not jaunting around South America without any serious purpose.

The following morning Naomi came to Sarah's house for their weekly conference. Most of the time they kept in touch electronically, often exchanging ten or twenty e-mails a day.

'You didn't tell me you had your sights on Royce Baring's company?' said Sarah, as she closed her office door.

'I didn't...until I met him. Then it struck me that if we could nobble him, everyone else in the Yellow Pages for this area would be easy-peasy.'

'I would think, if he wanted a website, he would go to one of the bigger operatives, not a couple of backroom girls.'

'That ain't necessarily so.' Naomi rummaged in her bag

for the phial of sweeteners she used in tea and coffee. They always started their chat session with a mug of de-caff. 'I've put the wind up Royce, telling him about all the cowboys there are in this business. Also he fancies me. I quite fancy him as a matter of fact. What did you think of him?'

'He has a lot of charm. Neal thought he looked like a wolf.'

'You know what they say...it takes one to know one. I couldn't believe my eyes when I saw your Neal.'

'Why...what do you mean?'

'You told me he was gorgeous, but I took that with a pinch of salt. Women in love always think their man is gorgeous, even if he's dead ordinary. The photo didn't do him justice—Neal really *is* that elusive ten-out-of-ten. I don't want to throw cold water, but I think you need to be totally realistic. Enjoy it while it lasts, but don't kid yourself it's for ever.'

Although she had always known it was part of Naomi's credo to say what she thought, even if her opinions were not always welcome, Sarah was shaken.

'I am realistic. I didn't expect to see him again after we said goodbye in Nepal. When he rang me from London, I more or less told him it was over. He wouldn't take no for an answer. He came here to arrange for me *and* Mum to visit his family.'

'I'm not saying he isn't mad about you, but mad may be the operative word. Men do go mad over women...and then, suddenly, their blood cools and they come to their senses. I don't want to see you hurt, Sarah. You've had enough hurts in your life.'

'Did Royce Baring make any comment...about the dif-ference in our ages?'

'No, but he felt *his* virility challenged. When you see him with the other town councillors, with their jowls and their bulging midriffs, Royce looks like a racehorse in a field of bullocks. But he doesn't look nearly as good standing next to your guy. That's why he whipped us away. He could feel his charisma being eclipsed.'

'Are you going to have an affair with him?' Sarah asked.

'Need you ask? He's good company. He's attractive. He'll give me a good time. I shall try very hard to convince him that I would be perfect as Mrs Royce Baring the second. But I know I'm not going to succeed. He will only marry again when he can't pull attractive women. Given his income, that might never come to pass.'

She drank some coffee, eyeing Sarah over the rim of the mug. 'It's no good pulling that face. That is the way the world is. Men, especially rich men, go on being attractive for ever. Women don't. In only a few more years, you and I will be past our sell-by date. So let's make hay while the sun shines but not kid ourselves that the harvest won't come to an end.'

The secret depression induced by Naomi's homily was still weighing on Sarah when she and her mother travelled by train to London.

Mrs Anderson took a child-like pleasure in the journey. She watched the passing scenery as intently as if it were some exotic landscape never glimpsed before. She enjoyed every mouthful of her lunch served by an attentive steward to whom she had artlessly confided that it was her first journey south.

When the train glided into one of London's main-line stations, she could hardly contain her excitement. At Neal's insistence, Sarah had rung him on her mobile to let him know the number of their carriage. The rest of the passengers had hardly disembarked before he was there, taking charge of the tricky business of helping her mother to negotiate the steps to platform level. He had already opened a folding wheelchair and had a porter waiting to handle their luggage while he wheeled Mrs Anderson through the bustling concourse and helped her into a taxi.

To Sarah, unaccustomed to having a man in charge, it was unbelievably effortless. Her downcast spirits began to rise, although she was still apprehensive about what his family would think of her.

As the taxi took them through the busy streets of the metropolis, Neal sat on the fold-down seat facing her mother, pointing out various landmarks. When, occasionally, he glanced at Sarah, there was a warmth in his eyes that made her wonder if Naomi's forecast could be wrong; if, somehow, against all reason, it was going to work out. Then, catching sight of a young man with wild hair and a knapsack slung over his shoulder, she remembered her son and the flash of optimism faded. What was Matthew going to think? What if he and Neal disliked each other on sight?

When the taxi drew up outside an imposing house in what seemed to Sarah a most elegant part of London, Neal said, 'You'll meet the rest of the family later. Right now I expect you'd like to freshen up and unpack.'

The lift he had mentioned whisked them from the hall to the upper floors. As soon as he had shown Mrs Anderson her room, he led Sarah along a short corridor to another bedroom. There he put her case down, closed the door and took her in his arms.

'Have you missed me?'

'Yes,' she admitted.

'Me too. Let's go to bed.'

'We can't—' she began, aghast, before she realised he was teasing.

'Perhaps not…but later…definitely!' His arms tightened, he pressed her against him, his kiss a promise of other kisses to come.

In one of the wild, wanton moments that he could

arouse in her, she was struck by an urgent longing to be loved…here and now. Sliding her arms round his neck, she ground her hips against his, knowing the effect it would have.

For a moment, but only a moment, it was she who was calling the shots. Then Neal answered her challenge. She found herself walked swiftly backwards until she could feel the edge of the divan against her legs.

He broke off the kiss to mutter a thick, 'God, I want you,' against the curve of her throat.

Then he recovered control. She knew the effort it cost him because, when she opened her eyes, his were still fierce slits of desire. But an instant later that had changed. He had his emotions in check, only the knot of muscle at the angle of his jaw betraying that letting her go was not what his inner self wanted.

Without the support of his arms, Sarah plumped down on the bed, feeling as if she had almost been caught by a whirlwind.

'I'll be back in about half an hour.' His voice still husky, Neal left.

Meeting his family proved less of an ordeal than she had imagined. In the ordinary way, she wouldn't have worried about it. It was only because of her relationship with Neal, and uncertainty about how her mother would cope with an unfamiliar environment and an embarrassment of strangers, that Sarah had butterflies inside her when Neal took them down to his parents' part of the house.

As it turned out, they both had engagements that afternoon and wouldn't be back until later. So the visitors had time to adjust to their new surroundings before meeting the people who had created them.

The huge room on the ground floor had several of the features Sarah had admired in the lounge of the hotel where Neal had stayed while visiting her. The walls were lined with books and pictures. The floor was laid with time-mellowed Eastern rugs. There were pot-plants and fresh flowers everywhere, many comfortable places to sit and a generally homely atmosphere combined with indications that the people who lived here were much better off and more sophisticated than the Andersons.

At one end of the room, tall windows screened for privacy by long folds of plain white net overlooked the street and another row of similar houses on the other side of it. At the other, glass doors led into a large conservatory beyond which could be seen a long narrow walled London garden with several mature trees.

A woman in an overall brought in a tea tray. Neal dealt with the pouring out as if there were nothing unusual about a man performing this service. Sarah could see that her mother found it astonishing. To her, men were the breadwinners and, when at home, were waited on by women. Even though Sarah had long been the family breadwinner, she knew that, when Matthew came back, her mother would defer to him more than to her and exert herself more for him.

They had finished tea and Neal was sitting next to Mrs Anderson, talking her through a large book of beautiful photographs of Kathmandu, when the door opened and a tall, slim woman came in. She was wearing trousers, a cashmere sweater and a jacket with a large clip on the lapel. Her dark hair, worn in a chignon, had a dramatic white streak.

'Sarah!' With hands outstretched, she crossed the room to where Sarah had turned from a painting she had been studying. 'I'm sorry I couldn't be here when you arrived. I've been so looking forward to meeting you.' She took both of Sarah's hands and squeezed them with firm, warm fingers.

When Neal introduced Mrs Anderson, his mother's manner was equally welcoming. But Sarah had the feeling that here was someone extremely clever and shrewd who would always be a gracious hostess but, if she found them wanting, would, with the utmost diplomacy, make that clear to her son.

Presently her husband joined them. He had features in common with his son, but the closest resemblance was between Neal and his grandfather who came in a little later to join them for pre-dinner drinks.

Still upright and keen of eye, the senior Mr Kennedy was a vision of what Neal would be like in extreme old age when time had wasted his strength and suppleness but left him with the fine bone structure that made his grandparent still a formidable presence.

'So you are the girl my grandson met in mid-air,' he said, after taking her arm and drawing her aside.

To him, she realised, she must look a girl. If only she were…

'Let's go and sit over there,' he said, indicating the sofa with its back to the street windows. 'Unfortunately I'm rather deaf and talking to more than one person at a time is difficult for me. I hear you're a Web designer. I spend a lot of time on the Internet. I've given up real world travel in favour of virtual globe-trotting. Tell me, what do you think about…?'

They were still deep in conversation when Neal came to replenish their glasses of white wine.

'I needn't ask what you two are gossiping about,' he said, smiling down at them.

His grandfather used the arm of the sofa to lever himself to his feet. 'I mustn't monopolise you, Sarah. I'll go and talk to your mother and give you and Neal a chance to exchange a few words before we have dinner.'

Taking his place, Neal said, 'I knew you two would hit it off. Are you feeling more relaxed now?'

'Didn't I look relaxed earlier?'

'Outwardly—yes. But when people know each other

well, they sense what's under the surface. When you first came down, you were a bundle of tension.'

At this point the woman in the overall came in and said, 'Dinner's ready when you are, Dr Kennedy.'

'We'll come at once, Mrs Haig.' Neal's mother indicated that everyone should follow her across the hall to a room with dark red walls.

The dining table was a round one. Sarah sat between Neal and his father, with her mother between him and his father.

The meal was unpretentious home cooking, with Mrs Haig placing the serving dishes in the centre of the table and everyone passing them round.

The first course was garlic mushrooms served in small brown ramekins, followed by fresh salmon steaks with baked potatoes and other vegetables. The pudding was baked apples with fromage frais.

Mrs Anderson always did full justice to her food, but Sarah was surprised at her mother's readiness to join in the conversation. Far from being shy, she was unusually animated, contributing more to the various discussions than Sarah herself did.

Later, when they were alone in her mother's bedroom, Mrs Anderson said, 'What a shame about their other son being killed.'

'Who told you that?'

'She did…Mrs Kennedy. When we were having coffee in the big room, I asked if she had other children. She said Neal had two sisters and an elder brother who'd died in a climbing accident.'

'Neal told me about him. I should have warned you, Mum.'

'It was some time ago. I expect she's learned to live with it. People have to, don't they? We've had our sorrows too.'

Sarah wondered if her mother could really count the

loss of her husband as a sorrow. Tonight she had glimpsed the woman her mother might have been if she hadn't spent years under the thumb of a domestic tyrant. How could she sincerely mourn a man who had done that to her?

Presently, in her own room, Sarah prepared for bed, wondering if Neal would come to her. She felt uneasy about sleeping with him under his parents' roof but knew that, if he did come, he would only have to kiss her to make her misgivings evaporate.

She was in bed, dipping into one of a stack of books on the night table, when there was a light tap at the door. She said a low-voiced, 'Come in.'

There was no suggestion of stealth about the way he walked in and closed the door.

'Did you enjoy the evening?' Neal spoke quietly but not in an undertone. He had been wearing a tie which he began to unwind as he crossed to the bed and sat down beside her.

'Yes, I did...and so did Mum. I've never seen her so animated. She doesn't normally drink wine so that may have had something to do with it.'

'She didn't have very much. It was probably more the effect of a complete change of scene and some new people to talk to. She's been in a rut. You both have. It's not a good place to be.'

He reached for one of her hands, turning it palm up and looking at the lines on it. 'Shall I tell you your fortune?'

Even this playful touch of his fingers was enough to quicken her pulses. 'Don't tell me you're a clairvoyant as well as a doctor and columnist.'

'I can foretell the immediate future. You're going to sleep well in spite of it being a strange bed. Tomorrow night you're going to have dinner alone with a man who thinks you are far more beautiful than you realise.'

'Oh, Neal...' Longing to tell him she loved him, she leaned forward to clasp her hands at the back of his neck.

The bedclothes, which had been pulled up to her chest, fell away. She was wearing a nightgown she had seen in a charity shop and been unable to resist. The top was made of exquisitely fine dove-grey lace, shaped to outline her breasts. The rest was pale peach silk-satin. It was a honeymoon nightie that, new, must have cost the earth. She had paid the price of four cups of coffee for it because, said the woman in the shop, some of their customers didn't like the idea of wearing what she had called 'other people's intimate garments'.

Sarah had had no such scruples. Very carefully, she had washed and pressed the luxurious garment, and now was rewarded by the way Neal was looking at her.

Gently, he took her wrists and drew them away from his neck and placed them on her lap. Then he took the fine rolled ribbon straps of the nightgown and edged them over the curves of her shoulders before slowly and carefully lowering the delicate lace as if he were peeling the skin of some rare exotic fruit.

The heat in his eyes and the controlled precision of his fingers made her tremble, her throat tight and dry with excitement while another part of her moistened and quivered in mounting anticipation.

Neal closed his eyes, his fingertips exploring her soft curves like those of a sightless person feeling the shape and smoothness of a sculpture.

Sarah's breathing quickened. Instinctively she arched her spine, her head falling back, her eyes closing in sensuous enjoyment.

And then, where his fingers had been, she felt first the warmth of his breath and, tantalising moments later, the warmer pressure of his lips. A shaft of intense physical pleasure shot through her body, making her give a long shuddering gasp.

Blindly she reached for his shoulders, needing something to cling to in the wild white water rush of feelings beyond her control.

The following evening, after a day spent showing Mrs Anderson some of the sights of London, Neal took Sarah to a small but elegant restaurant where they were shown to a table separated from its neighbours by partitions upholstered, like the banquettes, with dark green velvet.

Eating an avocado salad garnished with green olives stuffed with white cheese topped with glistening dark grains of caviare, Sarah said, 'It was kind of you to organise such a good sight-seeing tour for Mum. You must have seen all those places a hundred times.'

'I enjoyed seeing it through her eyes. Living in London, it's easy to become blasé. Another time I'll take you on a tour of my own favourite places, but I didn't think they were suitable for your mother's first circuit.'

'She's going to find life at home very dull after all this excitement.'

'Life doesn't have to be dull for anyone,' said Neal. 'I think she should be encouraged to be a lot more active both physically and mentally. Would you mind if I gave her a pep talk?'

'Of course not. In the past I have tried to get her to go to evening classes and so on. She's always resisted my efforts. Perhaps you can succeed where I failed.'

'It wouldn't surprise me if Grandpa took her to task while they're having supper together. He has a bee in his bonnet about people not wringing every last ounce of interest and enjoyment out of life. He hates the prospect of dying and missing all the exciting developments being forecast.'

'He's a wonderful old man…and you're going to be the same,' she said, smiling across the table. 'It's obvious you have a lot of his genes in you.'

'I'd like to think so.'

A waiter removed their plates and another refilled the wine glasses. For their main course they had both chosen poached fresh salmon.

Having eaten it, Sarah said, 'I don't think I can manage a pudding.'

'Nor can I. We'll have coffee, please,' Neal told the waiter.

When it had come, with a dish of hand-made chocolates, he said, 'I've been waiting for this moment all day. I've never been here before but I was told it was the right kind of place to ask the woman you love if she'll marry you. Will you, Sarah?'

CHAPTER TEN

IT TOOK several seconds for the momentous question to sink in. In unguarded moments she had let herself daydream about it, but never really believed it would happen.

Now it had and she didn't know what to say. In her heart, she wanted to say yes. But her head counselled caution. She was not, had never been truly independent. Before she was fully grown up and able to take control of her life, she had relinquished that freedom.

'You do love me, don't you?' Neal asked.

'You know I do,' she said quietly. 'But it isn't as simple as that. There are other people to consider.'

He was silent, watching her, his expression more guarded than a few moments earlier.

'Your parents have been very nice to me, but I can't believe that they aren't secretly concerned,' she went on. 'I might look a girl to your grandfather, but not to them. They must guess I'm older than you are.'

'My mother asked how old you were and what you looked like before she met you.'

'What did she say when you told her my age?'

'What would you expect her to say?'

'If Matthew was involved with a woman of forty, I'd try to dissuade him from getting too serious.'

'From what you tell me, Matthew hasn't got his own life together yet. It's important to do that before asking someone to share your life. I have. My mother knows that. She trusts my judgment. It would be nice if you did,' he added dryly.

'That's not quite fair. You know I trust you. I wouldn't have gone to Nagarkot if I hadn't. But nobody's judgment is sound when they're in the grip of... when they're feeling the way we both do at the moment.'

'I'm expecting to feel like this for the rest of my life.' He reached across the table to capture the hand with which she was fingering the stem of her wine glass. 'My parents' feelings have lasted. Why shouldn't ours?'

'Your parents were in their twenties when they got married. Your mother told Mum that and she passed it on to me when I was making her bed. They had no emotional baggage to complicate matters.'

'Are you saying that part of your heart still belongs to Matthew's father?'

'No, that's not what I meant at all. If it weren't for Matthew, I wouldn't remember clearly what Matt looked like. I think I was more in love with love than with him. If he hadn't been killed, if I hadn't had his baby, I would have grown out of loving him. That's the honest truth of it.'

'And now you're afraid that you'll grow out of loving me?'

'No,' she said vehemently. 'Never.' Then wished she had held her tongue. To try to persuade him to wait while admitting how much she cared for him was contradictory.

Quickly, before he could latch on to the inconsistency, she said, 'You've been very sweet to Mum, but having her for a few days isn't the same as having a mother-in-law on your hands for the rest of her life.'

Neal was still holding her hand. 'The time may come when my parents need looking after. Would that bother you?'

'That's different.'

'No, it isn't. The only important issue is whether you want to marry me. That's what you have to decide. Everything else is irrelevant.'

'Matthew isn't irrelevant. He's been the centre of my

life since I was eighteen...the person who kept me going when I felt it might never come right.'

'Irrelevant was the wrong word,' Neal conceded. 'Of course he and your mother are important to you...very important. But it's *your* life, *your* future we're talking about. Our future. I've waited a long time to find you and now that I have I don't want to hang about. I want us to be together all the time, not in snatches.'

'You make it sound so simple. It isn't. I have a business to run. I can't just walk out on Naomi. I wouldn't expect you to drop your column for *The Journal*.'

'I don't expect you to drop anything, Sarah. But you don't need to go on living where you are and neither do I. We can pick a place that we both like and work from there. That may take a little time to set up. Meanwhile I want to be able to call you my wife...to share a bedroom openly.'

'Neal, you're rushing me. I need more time. Until tonight I didn't know if you were serious, or if it was just an affair.'

'It was never "just an affair", but I knew you were hiding things from me. Now there are no more secrets, why must we wait?'

'I think you should meet my son, and Matthew needs to meet you. For him to come home, after a year away, and find me considering marriage...it would be a terrific shock. It could alienate him.'

Neal's lips compressed but he didn't say what he was thinking. She could guess what that was: that Matthew's reaction was a matter of indifference to him.

'Please...try to understand...try to be patient. There are so many complications. To rush into marriage would be madness.'

He let go of her hand and leaned back against the banquette.

'If that's the way you want it, that's how it will have

to be,' he said, with a slight shrug. 'When is he due to get home?'

'I'm not sure exactly. Before Christmas.'

'What do you do about Christmas? Link up with Naomi? Go to a hotel?'

'Naomi spends Christmas with her daughter. We spend it quietly at home. What do you do?'

'We have a big family Christmas, starting with a party for close friends the night before Christmas Eve. Why don't the three of you join us? There won't be room in the house because my sisters and their families will be staying with us, but there's a small hotel very near where you'd be comfortable. If you are going to marry me—subject to your son's approval—it would be a good time to get to know your future in-laws.'

'It's not a question of ''subject to my son's approval'',' Sarah said, in a low voice. 'But how would you feel, in his place, if you came home from abroad and found everything in upheaval and someone you'd never met taking over your mother's life...because that's how he'd be bound to see it. Children with only one parent are more possessive than children with two parents and brothers and sisters. It's inevitable. Except for his teachers, Matthew never had any masculine input in his early life.'

'That isn't going to happen now. He's a man, not a teenager. How he runs his life is his business, not mine. We're going to meet as equals, not in some quasi-stepfather-stepson relationship.'

As he spoke, Neal looked at his watch. 'If you've had enough coffee, let's go, shall we?' He signalled to their waiter.

While he paid the bill, Sarah was miserably aware that, by not giving him the unequivocal 'yes' he had expected and wanted, she had wounded him deeply. At the same time she found it hard to understand why he couldn't see the impossibility of doing that.

He dismissed the impediments to their marriage as if they were trivialities. But they weren't. Every day marriages foundered on much smaller obstacles to happiness.

They had walked to the restaurant and, the night being mild and dry, she had expected they would walk back. But outside the restaurant Neal raised his hand to a cruising taxi. As it drew up beside them, he opened the door for her and gave his address to the driver while she was stepping inside.

Throughout the short drive, they sat apart from each other, not speaking. It wasn't exactly a quarrel, but suddenly an abyss had opened between them and she didn't know how to bridge it.

Outside his house, Neal sprang out first and, turning, offered his hand to her. But she knew it had no significance. He had grown up under the influence of people with traditional ideas on good manners and chivalry towards women was as deeply ingrained in him as in his grandfather.

She waited while he paid the fare. As the cab drew away, she said, 'Thank you for taking me out, Neal. It was a delicious meal. I'm sorry that—'

He cut her short. 'We've talked it through. Let's give it a rest for a while.'

On the train going home, Mrs Anderson chattered almost without pause. Sarah listened and made a few comments but, although she tried to concentrate on what her mother was saying, her mind kept drifting away to dwell on how the situation would resolve itself.

Neal had kissed her goodbye, but only on the cheek. In the taxi to the station he had raised the subject of a London Christmas with her mother who, predictably, had been enthusiastic. But he hadn't come to Sarah's room the night before, nor had he said anything about when they would next see each other. She had hated saying goodbye with the abyss still yawning between them, even if the Christmas plan was intended as a bridge.

It was only towards the end of the journey that it struck her as strange that her mother, who by now had recapped almost every moment of the visit, had said nothing about the reason for it. Surely she must realise there was more than friendship between them?

At that moment, as if their mental processes had somehow become linked, Mrs Anderson said, 'I thought, when he took you out last night, Neal might be going to pop the question. Anyone can see he's keen on you.'

'If he did, what would you want me to say, Mum?'

'It's not what I want, it's what you want that matters. I'd miss you, I can't deny it. But the way we live isn't right, not for someone of your age. You need a man in your life…a nice man who'll be kind to you. When I married your father, I didn't realise it's kindness that counts in the long run. I was bowled over by his looks. I didn't think about his nature. Your Neal's got both…looks and a nice nature.'

'He's not my Neal, Mum. Did his mother say anything to you…about him and me?'

'Nothing direct, but I could tell that she liked you. So she should. You're solid gold, Sarah, and I don't say that just because I'm your mum. There's lots of girls, left as you were, who'd have dumped the baby on me and gone off and had a good time. And that's what you deserve to have from now on. You've had your share of hard times. You deserve to be happy from now on.'

'Do you think Matthew will like Neal?'

Her mother considered the question. 'I expect he'll be jealous at first. That's only natural. He's always come first with you. It'll take time for him to get used to coming second.'

'I wonder how much he'll have changed?' Sarah said

thoughtfully. 'I'm hoping he'll have grown up. He wasn't very mature when he went away.'

That evening, Neal rang to check that their return had gone smoothly.

'Was there any news from Matthew when you got home?' he asked.

'Not yet. I'm just writing a thank-you letter to your parents,' said Sarah.

'I'll call you tomorrow. Goodnight.'

'Goodnight,' she echoed, hurt by the brevity and businesslike tone of the call, but knowing she had inflicted a much greater hurt on him by responding to his proposal with caution instead of the eagerness he had wanted and expected.

'Neal, something is wrong,' said Mrs Kennedy, the next time she and her son were alone together. 'I've tried not to intrude in any of your lives since you've been adults, but perhaps if I'd asked Chris about his problems instead of maintaining my policy of non-interference...' She left the rest in the air.

It was years since Neal had confided his troubles to either of his parents, largely because none had arisen that he couldn't handle. He had no doubt he could deal with the present imbroglio, but his mother's slant on it might be worth hearing. He outlined the situation.

Liz Kennedy listened in silence. After some thought, she said, 'I took to Sarah from the moment we met and this confirms my opinion. She's right to face up to the special problems that exist. It sounds to me as if she loves you enough to want what's best for you and to put that ahead of what's best for her. If you marry her, it's unlikely you'll have children. Not impossible...but not likely.'

'That's not an issue.'

'Not for you perhaps...but it may be for her. The least

maternal of women tend to want to have a child by a man they love.'

'Sarah has a child by her first love. I'm happy to be her last love...with or without any offspring.'

'Then the only possible obstacle to your happiness is her existing offspring. The bond between them is bound to be very strong, perhaps stronger than it should be, given the circumstances. For single parents like Sarah, it must be difficult not to become too close. Parents like Dad and me have each other to turn to when our children fly the nest. When a marriage is strong, it's good to have time and space to concentrate on the person you started out with.'

Neal smiled at her. 'Dad's a lucky guy.'

'We're both lucky,' said Mrs Kennedy. 'I want the same luck for you. Chris's marriage seemed to have all the ingredients for success, but it was a disaster. On the face of it, some people might think Sarah wasn't the right woman for you, but I have the feeling she is.'

After a pause, she added, 'And however difficult and antagonistic her son may be, I'm sure you can handle him.'

'He may not be difficult at all,' said Neal.

'I think that would be too much to hope for,' said his mother.

When, three weeks after the visit to London, there was still no word from Matthew, Sarah began to feel annoyed with both the men in her life.

Everyone else's mind was focused on Christmas, but she found it impossible to think about anything but when she would see Neal again and when her son would turn up.

Neal rang her almost every evening, but said nothing about their next meeting. Matthew didn't call or send an e-mail. Anything might have happened to him.

'He's a wretch to worry you and your mother like this,' Naomi said crossly. 'Travel may broaden the mind but it doesn't appear to have made him more considerate. As for Neal, why can't you tell him you're dying to see him?'

'For the same reason you won't tell Royce you'd like to be Mrs Baring unless he suggests it,' said Sarah. 'We may be post-feminist women, but there are still some areas where we want men to take the lead. Neither Neal nor Royce is the bashful type. If they *don't* take the initiative, it's reasonable to assume that they don't want the same thing we want.'

'I don't know about Royce, but if Neal is still keeping in touch on an almost daily basis, he's not cooling off,' said Naomi.

That evening, about the time when Neal usually called her, Sarah's door bell rang. It was Friday. Her heart leapt in hope that it might be Neal, coming to spend the weekend with her.

She flew downstairs to open the door. For a moment her heart plummeted for it wasn't Neal on the doorstep, but a man she wouldn't have known if she'd passed him in a crowded street, without the large rucksack he had dumped on the step.

A mane of dark curly hair tied back at his nape and a neatly trimmed naval beard framed a face with a mariner's tan that was almost unrecognisably thinner than the face last seen in January.

'Hi, Mum. How's it going?'

Matthew stepped over the threshold and enveloped her in a bear hug.

Sarah burst into tears of joy and relief.

The telephone started ringing.

'Hadn't you better answer it?' Matthew suggested, releasing her.

Blinking, fumbling for a handkerchief, Sarah went to

the kitchen where there was a wall-hung receiver. 'Hello?' she said huskily.

'It's Neal. Is something the matter?'

She was surprised he had picked up the vibes so quickly. 'No, everything's fine. I just opened the door and found Matthew outside. Can I call you back later?'

'Of course. Tomorrow will do…when you come down from cloud nine. Bye.' He rang off.

'Was that Naomi? How is she?' Matthew asked. He had heaved his pack over the threshold and dumped it against the panelling at the side of the stairs.

'She's fine. It was someone else. Come and say hello to Gran. She'll be so relieved to see you. We've been worried about you.'

'Women! They're always worrying!' Cheerfully dismissing their anxiety, Matthew opened the door of the lounge. 'Still addicted to soaps, then, Gran?' he said, with a grin. 'Shall I keep out till it's over?'

His grandmother gave a shriek, zapped the domestic drama taking place on the screen and opened her arms to him.

The following evening, while Matthew was out seeing friends, Sarah called Neal.

After some conversation, he asked, 'Have you told him about us?'

'Not yet. There hasn't been time. There's been so much we wanted to hear about his adventures.'

'I'll drive up early next Saturday and take you all out to lunch. That should give you plenty of time to tell him your news,' said Neal.

Taking her agreement for granted, he said he was busy writing an urgently-needed commentary on the sudden illness of a showbiz star, and brought the call to an end.

Sarah was cooking things for the freezer when Matthew came in. Having him at home meant a lot more food was needed. There had been a time when, although she was busy, he would have expected her to break off and make coffee for him. Now he made some for both of them.

'You look tired, Mum...you work too hard. This will give you a buzz: I've got myself a job...starting Monday.'

While he told her about it, Sarah sipped her coffee and braced herself for telling him her news. She was pleased by the change in his attitude. He did seem a lot more mature, but would his new outlook stretch to encompassing her marriage to a thirtysomething?

Matthew had already heard about her trip to Nepal but not about Neal. When the moment came, she said, 'I hope you're free on Saturday because someone I met in Nepal wants the three of us to have lunch with him. Gran has already met him. They get on very well.'

'Don't tell me you've found her a boyfriend? I thought she seemed a lot more lively. What's he like?'

'His name is Neal Kennedy. He's a qualified doctor but he works as a medical journalist.'

'If he's making enough to go on expensive trips, maybe he can afford to take Gran off your hands,' he said jokingly. 'That would be brilliant. She's a dear old stick, but a bit of a weight round your neck.'

'Actually it's me he's interested in. He...he wants to marry me, Matthew.'

Predictably, he looked flabbergasted. After a long pause, he said, 'That's quick work, isn't it?'

'Nothing is signed and sealed yet. I wanted to wait until you got back.'

'Well...if it's what you want, I guess it's OK by me...but a retired doctor seems kind of old for you.'

'He's not retired,' she explained. 'Actually he's younger than I am.'

'Oh, right. That's better than a near-geriatric stepfather.' Matthew, whose body clock was still on South American time, opened the fridge and foraged for something to eat.

'So is he second time around? Are you going to have to be stepmum to his children?'

By the time Sarah went to bed, she had answered a lot of questions and Matthew seemed to have accepted the presence of a man in her life. But she knew that the moment of truth would be when he met Neal face to face.

On Saturday morning, she waited for Neal's arrival in a fever of mingled longing and apprehension. It seemed an age since she had felt his arms round her, but how would Matthew react if she spent the night at Neal's hotel? But it might never come to that. They might dislike each other on sight. Then what?

When she went downstairs after changing into a silk shirt and fine black wool trousers, she found that Matthew had also changed. Since coming home he had had his hair cut and shaved off his beard. Now he was wearing his grey interview suit with a conservative shirt and tie.

Which could only mean he was anxious to make a good impression on Neal, she realised, with a thrust of hope that the meeting would pass off smoothly.

'Sounds like a car,' said Matthew, going to the window. 'Yep, looks like your boyfriend.'

As Sarah went into the hall, her mother glided downstairs on the chair-lift. Sarah opened the front door, oblivious to the cold air as she saw Neal opening the gate, turning her weak at the knees.

He was carrying a large pot plant in a protective shield of transparent paper.

'It's seemed a long time,' he said, pausing to kiss her cheek before entering the hall and placing the plant on the table before embracing Mrs Anderson.

'Come along in and meet Matthew.' It was she who performed the introduction while Sarah stood in the background, wondering if one day her son would have the air of authority and the easy charm of the man she was in love with.

She had thought that Matthew would be visibly disconcerted by the fact that Neal was a lot younger than herself. But, if he was, it didn't show. Perhaps, being still in his twenties, her son saw Neal as a much older man.

Remembering the plant he had brought, she fetched it and placed it on the coffee table.

'I hope you like azaleas, Mrs Anderson?' he said, as Sarah unwrapped it.

'It's for me? It's beautiful. I've never seen such a big one. That lovely deep pink is my favourite colour. That is kind of you, Neal.'

'My pleasure. If everyone's ready, we may as well head for the hotel.'

In the car, the two men sat in front. They both had brown necks and dark hair. Although Matthew's was naturally curly like his father's, while Neal's was almost straight, they could easily have been taken for brothers.

While they were talking about cars, Mrs Anderson touched Sarah's arm and made faces indicating that they seemed to be hitting it off. Sarah responded by crossing her second fingers over her forefingers.

A few minutes later she saw Neal looking at her in the rear-view mirror. It was only a momentary meeting of eyes but it seemed to send her a message that he couldn't wait to be alone with her. She longed to reach out and lay her hand on his shoulder.

At the hotel, they had drinks in the bar before moving to the restaurant where the head waiter ushered them to what was obviously one of the best tables.

They were being presented with menus when the wine waiter arrived with one of his juniors wheeling a small trolley on which was an ice bucket containing a bottle of champagne. The wine waiter showed Neal the label. Sarah recognised the famous name. Could it be his intention to force her hand by announcing their impending marriage? Surely not? As they hadn't had any private conversation, he couldn't even be sure she had told Matthew how things stood.

'Are we celebrating something?' her mother asked archly, as a crystal flute filled with the pale golden wine was placed in front of her.

Inwardly Sarah groaned.

'Your grandson's safe return from his travels,' said Neal. He raised his own glass to Matthew. 'In my view, everyone should go off and see the world before settling down. I notice a big difference between people who've done it and those who haven't. They're more self-reliant, more capable, more open-minded. To Matthew and his well-spent year.'

Infinitely relieved, Sarah beamed at her son, proudly repeating the toast before putting her glass to her lips.

'Thanks very much,' Matthew said, looking slightly abashed at being toasted.

'I was talking to a TV presenter the other day,' Neal continued. 'When he was eighteen, Voluntary Service Overseas sent him to Africa to teach in a secondary school. He said it transformed him. But his most telling comment was, "I'd rather be stuck on a raft with someone who's done VSO than someone who hasn't."'

'Which presenter was it?' asked Mrs Anderson. When he told her, she said, 'Oh, he's one of my heart-throbs.'

'I enquired about VSO before I took off,' said Matthew. 'Now they only take people with special qualifications, so I went off my own bat.'

Encouraged by Neal to talk about his adventures, he produced several anecdotes the two women hadn't heard before.

'You ought to write about your trip. There's always a market for really good travellers' tales. It helps to have some contacts. Perhaps I could steer you in one or two useful directions.'

'Would you?' Matthew asked eagerly. 'I'd like to have a crack at journalism. It's the only career that really appeals to me, but everyone says it's next to impossible to break into it.'

'Nothing's impossible if it's what you really want,' said Neal. He switched his gaze to Sarah and gave her a smile of such clear meaning that she felt the others must read it.

Towards the end of the meal, before the coffee was served, Mrs Anderson asked Sarah to help her to walk to the Ladies.

'I'm so pleased they're getting on nicely,' she said, on the way there.

'It's early days yet, Mum.'

'You worry too much, love. I knew it would all work nicely.'

Perhaps she was right, Sarah thought hopefully as, on their way back to the table, she saw the two men deep in conversation.

As the women approached, they both rose, Matthew to push in his grandmother's chair for her. Neal didn't move to do the same for Sarah. In fact he blocked her way to it.

Taking her hand in a firm clasp, he looked down at her mother. 'We'll see you later, Mrs A. Matthew will explain the arrangements.'

Transferring Sarah's hand to his right hand and putting his left hand at her waist, he led her away from the table.

'Where are we going?' she demanded.

'I'm kidnapping you,' he said, smiling down at her. 'Instead of staying here for the weekend, I've booked a room at a place in the country. It's only an hour's drive. Matthew will take your mother home. He's more than capable of looking after her for a couple of nights.'

By now they were near the tall double doors where a waiter was holding the coat Sarah had handed over when they arrived.

'I hope you enjoyed your lunch, madam?' he said, as he held it for her to put on.

'Very much, thank you.' She gave him an abstracted smile.

To Neal, as he recaptured her hand, she said, 'But I haven't any clothes.'

'You won't need any. We're going to spend the entire weekend in bed...making up for lost time. Then we're going to get married. I've asked your son for his approval and he's given it.'

'What did you say? What did he say?'

'I said I loved you and wanted to share lives with you. He said it was a great idea. It would get you off his back. He qualified that by saying that he loved you too, but you and his grandmother were a pair of world-class fusspots and a guy of his age doesn't need that. He also said it would be good to have another man in the family to re-dress the present imbalance.'

Sarah's mind was in such confusion that her thoughts had no logical sequence. She said, 'Couldn't we stop off at the house to pick up some country shoes? We can't spend *all* day in bed. We might want to go for a walk.'

'If you're in it, I can easily spend all day in bed. But if you insist, we'll stop off.'

By now they were outside the building, heading for his car.

'What about the bill for lunch?' she exclaimed. 'Matthew may not have enough money to pay it.'

'He won't need to. I paid it with plastic when you left the table. Everything is taken care of. You can empty your head of all worries and think of nothing but this.'

Instead of unlocking the car, he sandwiched her between the side of it and his tall powerful body. Taking her face in his hands, he said, 'I need you, Sarah. I've never felt, or expected to feel, this way about a woman before. We belong together. You know we do.'

The depth of feeling in his voice made her tremble with longing to believe him. To throw away the fear in the corner of her mind that, always, however happy they were, she would worry about the day when she would no longer be desirable.

And then, looking into his eyes, she had a moment of almost blinding enlightenment, seeing how foolish it was to hold back from happiness because of a distant eventuality that might never come.

Life was so fragile, so fleeting. She, more than most people, had reason to know that tomorrow might never come.

Neal loved and needed her *now*. The future was unimportant compared with the present.

'I know we do,' she said softly. 'Oh, Neal, what a fool I was not to see that before. I was trying to be wise and sensible. I'm sorry I hurt you, my dear love.'

Regardless of who might be watching, she gripped the lapels of his jacket and reached up to kiss him, closing her eyes as she felt his eager response.

Presently, reluctantly, they drew apart. Neal unlocked the car and put her into it. As he slid into the driver's seat, he leaned over and gave her another quick kiss before fastening his seat belt and switching on the engine.

'Where is this place you're taking me?' she asked, as he backed the car.

'Wait and see,' he said, his attention on what he was doing, but a smile lurking round his mouth. 'I promise you it will be a lot more comfortable than Nagarkot.'

'I loved Nagarkot. I was very happy there…even though, at the time, I thought it was just a naughty weekend as far as you were concerned.'

'I wasn't sure that you didn't see it that way. We were both wrong.'

As he changed into first, Sarah looked at the strong but gentle hand on the gear lever and then at the forceful profile of the man beside her. She gave a sigh of contentment and settled back in her seat to enjoy the rest of this wonderful day and look forward to the night.

EPILOGUE

THREE months later, on the afternoon before their wedding, Neal drove her out of London to the village where they would live when they returned from their honeymoon.

Although their future home was called Fig Tree Cottage, it was actually a row of cottages which had been knocked into one low, rambling house. Since they had bought it, it had been rearranged yet again and was now two separate dwellings, one for them and one for Sarah's mother and a live-in carer, a kind and capable woman who had been found by Neal's mother.

The plan was that Neal and Sarah would live at his flat in London during the week, spending weekends in the country. That way they would be in close touch with her mother but not so close as to cause any friction.

This afternoon they were taking some wedding presents to the cottage. Although it was going to be a simple ceremony, there would be a lot of people present because Neal had numerous friends who would have been offended at being excluded.

During the drive down, Sarah remembered that she hadn't read Neal's latest column in today's issue of *The Journal*. It was lying on the back seat. She reached behind her for it, then searched the awkwardly large pages until she spotted his photograph and by-line. She folded the paper into a convenient size and started to read. Neal was playing a tape but had all his attention on the road because it was raining heavily. But tomorrow evening they would be flying to a Caribbean island, Anguilla, which the newspaper's travel editor had assured them was still unspoiled by mass tourism.

The column began with a piece about dealing with nose bleeds, went on to discuss remedies for fungal nail infections and ended with some comments on ways of dealing with infertility. It was this last section that activated the one last doubt still lurking in Sarah's mind.

She didn't read the rest of the paper but replaced it on the back seat and sat deep in thought. Without her noticing, both the music and the rain stopped. She only became aware of this when Neal said, 'You're very quiet, darling. Are you tired?'

There had been a lot to do in recent weeks, but it hadn't tired her. She had never felt more alive and energetic.

'No...I feel fine,' she said, trying to shrug off her secret anxiety, but not entirely succeeding.

'Something's the matter...tell me.'

The longer they were together, the more quickly he sensed what was going on in her mind. This particular concern was one they had already talked about, Neal being adamant that he wouldn't let her take the chance of having a baby, both for her own sake and also that of the child. As a doctor he knew the risks. That some women older than Sarah had had no problems didn't alter his view.

'You're not still worrying about the baby business, are you?' he asked.

'I can't help it,' she admitted. 'I'm sure you'd feel the same if the situation were reversed...if I were still in my thirties and you were unable to give me a child.'

'I'd take it for granted that, if you told me you loved me, you meant it. Nothing else mattered. I'd also assume you were mature enough to know that no one is *entitled* to anything. Compared with a lot of people around the world, we're damn lucky if we have a few good things in our lives. It's childish and selfish to expect everything.'

'I know that, but still—'

'Listen to me, Sarah. I want you…only you. For all I know I may be infertile. But if I am, and even if you were younger, I wouldn't expect it to worry you. It may not be long before Matthew falls in love and fathers some children. Meanwhile we have my sisters' brood around. So put this out of your mind and concentrate on all we have going for us. It's a lot.'

The firmness, almost sternness, of his tone finally convinced her. She saw what a burden it would be for him if she went on fretting and worrying about something that couldn't be altered.

'You're right,' she said, in a positive tone. 'Believe me, I know how lucky I am.'

'How lucky we both are,' he corrected.

Sarah had given a great deal of thought to her wedding outfit. Eventually she had chosen a very simple ankle-length cream silk suit and a cream straw picture hat with the front of the brim swept back so that it wouldn't get in the way when the moment came for their first married kiss.

She walked up the aisle of the small London church near where the Kennedys lived on the arm of her son, with Neal's eldest niece walking sedately behind them, thrilled at this opportunity to be a bridesmaid, being the only one among her schoolfriends who hadn't played this role before.

The Kennedy guests were occupying both sides of the aisle because there were many of them and not many Anderson guests. Naomi, to her own and Sarah's surprise, was accompanied by Royce Baring. They had both thought that weddings were occasions he would prefer to avoid.

Sarah's wish, as she smiled at them on her way to where Neal was waiting for her, was that one day Naomi would feel as happy and secure as she herself was feeling.

'You look gorgeous, Mum,' Matthew had told her, in the vestibule of the church.

He was looking very good himself, in a new suit bought on the strength of a job on a trade magazine that Neal had engineered for him.

Never having known what it was like to have someone ready and willing to take all her problems onto his much broader shoulders, Sarah still wasn't used to being lavished with tender loving care.

At the chancel steps, she removed her hand from her son's arm and Matthew stepped aside to make way for his soon-to-be stepfather. Sarah looked up into the smiling grey eyes of the man she loved.

She was on the threshold of a future that, a few months ago, she wouldn't have believed was possible. Since her meeting with Neal, there had been many sleepless nights; some spent in his arms, some alone, racked by worries and uncertainties.

Tonight would be another sleepless night because they were crossing the Atlantic on a flight that didn't take off till late in the evening. Perhaps they would doze a little. Perhaps they would talk. They had so much to talk about, so much still to discover.

Together they faced the parson who was going to marry them. But, in their hearts, all the vows had already been made.

MILLS & BOON®

Next Month's Romance Titles

———— ♡ ————

Each month you can choose from a wide variety of romance novels from Mills & Boon®. Below are the new titles to look out for next month from the Presents™ and Enchanted™ series.

Presents™

THE MISTRESS ASSIGNMENT	Penny Jordan
THE VIRGIN BRIDE	Miranda Lee
THE SEDUCTION GAME	Sara Craven
ONE WEDDING REQUIRED!	Sharon Kendrick
LUC'S REVENGE	Catherine George
THE MARRIAGE TAKEOVER	Lee Wilkinson
THE PLAYBOY'S BABY	Mary Lyons
HIRED WIFE	Karen van der Zee

Enchanted™

BOARDROOM PROPOSAL	Margaret Way
DR. TEXAS	Debbie Macomber
THE NINE-DOLLAR DADDY	Day Leclaire
HER HUSBAND-TO-BE	Leigh Michaels
THE FATHERHOOD SECRET	Grace Green
A WIFE AND CHILD	Rosemary Carter
A REAL ENGAGEMENT	Marjorie Lewty
WIFE WITHOUT A PAST	Elizabeth Harbison

On sale from 2nd April 1999

H1 9903

Available at most branches of WH Smith, Tesco, Asda, Martins, Borders, Easons, Volume One/James Thin and most good paperback bookshops

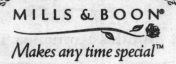

MILLS & BOON®

Makes any time special™

By Request

Bestselling themed romances brought back to you by popular demand

Each month By Request brings you three full-length novels in one beautiful volume featuring the best of the best.

So if you missed a favourite Romance the first time around, here is your chance to relive the magic from some of our most popular authors.

Look out for
Sole Paternity **in March 1999**
featuring Miranda Lee, Robyn Donald
and Sandra Marton

Available at most branches of WH Smith, Tesco,
Asda, Martins, Borders, Easons,
Volume One/James Thin
and most good paperback bookshops

FREE
4 BOOKS
AND A SURPRISE GIFT!

We would like to take this opportunity to thank you for reading this Mills & Boon® book by offering you the chance to take FOUR more specially selected titles from the Enchanted™ series absolutely FREE! We're also making this offer to introduce you to the benefits of the Reader Service™—

★ FREE home delivery   ★ FREE gifts and competitions
★ FREE monthly Newsletter   ★ Exclusive Reader Service discounts
★ Books available before they're in the shops

Accepting these FREE books and gift places you under no obligation to buy; you may cancel at any time, even after receiving your free shipment. Simply complete your details below and return the entire page to the address below. *You don't even need a stamp!*

YES! Please send me 4 free Enchanted books and a surprise gift. I understand that unless you hear from me, I will receive 6 superb new titles every month for just £2.40 each, postage and packing free. I am under no obligation to purchase any books and may cancel my subscription at any time. The free books and gift will be mine to keep in any case.

N9EC

Ms/Mrs/Miss/Mr ....Initials ....
BLOCK CAPITALS PLEASE
Surname..
Address...

....

....Postcode ....

Send this whole page to:
THE READER SERVICE, FREEPOST CN81, CROYDON, CR9 3WZ
(Eire readers please send coupon to: P.O. BOX 4546, DUBLIN 24.)

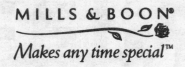

MILLS & BOON®

Makes any time special™

The Regency Collection

Mills & Boon® is delighted to bring back, for a limited period, 12 of our favourite Regency Romances for you to enjoy.

These special books will be available for you to collect each month from May, and with two full-length Historical Romance™ novels in each volume they are great value at only £4.99.

Volume One available from 7th May